VAMPIRES AT SEA

VAMPIRES AT SEA

LINDSAY MERBAUM

Sonya,

Thank you so much for coming to my
event! I hope you enjoy this little
"vacation." Cheers!

Creature Publishing
Charlottesville, VA

ISBN 9781951971229
LCCN 2024948331

Cover design by Jaya Nicely and artwork "The Fall of the Rebel Angels" by Pieter Bruegel the Elder
Spine illustration by Rachel Kelli

CREATUREHORROR.COM
@creaturepublishing

For all the hot queer sluts. You know who you are.

". . . all bad stories can become good stories if you line up the words right."

—Shilo Niziolek, *Fever*

"You will think me cruel, very selfish, but love is always selfish; the more ardent the more selfish. How jealous I am you cannot know."

—Joseph Sheridan Le Fanu, *Carmilla*

DAY 1

Our first night aboard the *Zorya*, the dark-sea wind fills our mouths and bloats our bellies. We're impaled on swords of artificial light. It's loud—the ship itself moans and hums. The *Zorya* looks like an obscene confection on a cushion of black velvet; I can't tell where the sky ends and the black sea begins. It is the Black Sea, actually, its depths the host for a discount cruise for classy art queers. The wind plucks at laughter and small talk. There are flirting sounds, clumsy quaffs of free champagne. *We're on vacation!* We queued for what felt like an eternity just to board this ship, corralled amongst our fellow passengers, who generated screechy chatter with their phones while moving as slowly as they possibly could toward our collective destination. When one dared to pop their gum, I shot them a look that could level a village.

"*Paciencia, mi zorrita,*" Hugh cautioned, taking my hand. His patience is infinite.

Fireworks pop off in the shape of a rainbow, then a unicorn. There are startled faces, expressions of delight. Soon, the slow, delicious selection process will begin, delicious to me, anyway. Who is worthy of a fuck and feed? There are thousands of them, all crammed aboard with nowhere to go. No escape. The maze at the center of the ship is windowless.

Hugh looks boyish, his black hair mussed. He's dashing too—a polyglot Argentine prince. He's especially dashing when he squints, in fact; Hugh's a sexy brooder. I think it's his shelf of a brow or his nose, the Romanesque severity they lend his profile. He has on a jacket and button-down, his usual uniform, with his suede vacation loafers. Some of his shoes are one of a kind, hand-stitched by people who are just bone dust now. The bright, rubbery bracelet thing we all have to wear is an insult to his thick hairy wrist.

Hugh's name is Hugo, but I decided at some point to call him Hugh, after Anaïs Nin's better-known husband. He doesn't mind. We've been together for hundreds of years, it feels like. Or maybe it really is. Who could say? You go through uncountable little moments, thousands of dawns, thousands of twilights, a hundred thousand miseries and feasts and feuds. If you remembered everything, you'd lose your mind.

Memory is a lie anyway. Half of what you remember is just what you imagine. You swear on your life your mother's house is sage green. But it isn't green, it's blue.

Or there is no house. It's a grave and the stone is gray and eroded. No mother either. Just you. And you don't even know what you're doing there.

We are on this cruise because some recently forged memories are a little too fresh in our minds. Let's just say I had a lover—which was fine. Hugh knew all about it, but things got a little out of hand. There was an escalation and a small fire—no, not a metaphoric one—and now Hugh is ruffled. He doesn't like to be ruffled. He likes me to do as I like. He likes to watch me do as I like. But loud noises, extreme temperatures, insistent voices, and destruction of his work are all things that make him nervous. He is, in general, anxious, reticent, qualities veiled by a slow, elegant manner. A finger held at the chin, the graceful way he crosses his legs so you can't help but wonder about his cock. (Length: moderate. Thick around the middle. Circumcised, surprisingly. Somewhat shy, but steadfast. In other words, perfect.) My drama passes through our home like a noxious vapor. Hugh, unmoored, locks himself in the bathroom. Sometimes he climbs out the window. Sometimes he doesn't come back.

Then, like a sign from the god I don't need to believe in: a coupon for a queer Black Sea cruise arrives folded up with the junk mail. With no sense of irony whatsoever, the coupon assures me this adventure is not for the everyday cruiser. This cruise itself is a work of art. Queer art. Also, there are actual works of art aboard the ship, I discover, when I visit the cruise line's website. I scan pictures of hordes of chemically uninhibited bodies with cellulite looking for pleasure, debasing themselves publicly, grinning, with drinks and sandwiches in their mitts. *The ocean! Europe! Horny lonely people!* This could work. I leave the brochure on the table, where I know Hugh will see it.

We don't actually need a coupon to go on a cruise. We don't need a cruise either. We could fly to Europe, rent a car, do whatever we like. But Hugh is as frugal as English royalty—I hear the Brits wear their moldy old suits for decades, and Hugh is just the same. Everything's tailored, dry-cleaned, polished, pickled, and preserved. Worth a small fortune to a monger of vintage clothing. Money is vanity of the wrong kind in Hugh's book. It's a heavy, moldering book.

People are always offering Hugh money, which embarrasses him. Grants, fellowships, and, worst of all, speaking tours. He deflects and dodges. He shudders at the very notion of a microphone. So Hugh has a reputation for being reclusive, which only makes him all the more desirable. But what would we do with money, really? We can have anything we want.

Personally, I do enjoy rich people. The delectable perfume of their avarice. I find satisfaction in their lust for wealth, but much more pleasure in their lust for me—ideally, I get both. Their pupils dilate as I foretell their investments' future. Ardor drips like honey from their fingertips into my waiting mouth. Investors offer me millions, and I give them promises, send them home semi-conscious in rideshares with their flies undone. What imbeciles. The actual cash is nothing to me, though it's everything to my starchy, soulless employers. It's a symbiotic relationship.

Sometimes there are literal cheers when I enter the office, and that does give me a little boost. I wear skirts that show off my legs, chic blouses and blazers. Classic. Every single officemate has tried to fuck me at one holiday party or another, where there's always a mini menorah, which they believe is for me. I suppose it's the rather Hebraic spelling of my name—Rebekah. A few get lucky. But I like best the peculiar tang of the longing coming off those I don't choose.

A petite Filipino man with a fixed smile shows us to our stateroom. I think his name is Stewart, but no, it turns out he *is* a steward. His name is . . . Ragnar? Remington? Something Germanic with an *R*. It doesn't matter. He has an irritating habit, a nervous cough I could exert my influence to disabuse him of, but I have more important concerns. First among them, our cabin is a closet, and the carpet is thin and rough, the sheets, too, serrated with sand. A small plexiglass plug the size of a toilet hole is pretending to be a window. And it smells like cigarettes, chlorine, mildew, desperation. Any thought of fucking evaporates. This cabin isn't even worth a rub-out.

Gingerly Hugh perches on the bed. He makes a face like he wishes he'd put a towel down first. Then he crosses his legs and clears his throat. "Well," he says. His hands unfold like lilies.

"We need an upgrade," I tell R the Steward, who's sweating. He starts explaining in his apologetic way that he is not authorized to approve upgrades, we'll have to speak to Goth Services. No, it's Guest Services. R says it like someone's name—Guest Services III. Fine then.

Hugh frowns. He is feigning hesitation and we both know it. He doesn't want to want what he wants. Oh, it's so tiresome, his self-loathing. I lick my lips and count the seconds, my way of practicing the patience I don't have.

Finally, Hugh relents.

R guides us through the thin passageways and down the elevator's throat to a tall half-moon desk with two dykes behind it who look like they could build a fire and fix your laptop at the same time. Their eyes light up at the sight of me because I'm hot as fuck. All it takes is a smile. They're gone before I even open my mouth.

Within fifteen minutes, we're lying in a champagne bed shaped like a clam in an ocean-view stateroom. Everything is champagne: the carpet, the walls. There's a bottle of it in a basket on the desk, in fact. This room has a settee, and a small tub with jets.

"*Bien hecho*," Hugh says. Now that the unpleasant part is over, he's content.

I want him to fuck me on the bed. He wants to fuck in the tub, but the tub is too small. It's impractical— where would my knees go? So I knock him to the floor and straddle him and my hips go to work. He forgets the tub, moaning, rubbing his hair into the sparkling-wine carpet as I ride his cock into oblivion.

In my earlier years, before I figured out how to properly nourish myself, I fed lazily, wantonly, indiscriminately; sampling desires, longings, obsessions, and other delicacies. I binged, seeking ecstasy. I nearly achieved it a few times. Then I found better ways. But I have no regrets.

We leave our bags unpacked and head for the entertainment arena on the upper deck, to pick out the nicest bar our wristbands will grant us entry to. We are celebrities under house arrest.

I ease in. The smile, the eye contact—held just a little too long. The tilt of my head reeling them closer. You can't break free even if you want to, which you don't. You're listening intently. I'm telling the most fascinating story you've ever heard. You can't believe it, your mouth is open to catch my every word like a pearl, a delicious pearl that cracks like candy between your molars. *What luck that we're meeting! And so soon into the trip!* The cologne you're wearing smells like money. Your watch is simple, understated, yet worth as much as a shitty studio in a neglected part of the city where we live. The younger one touches my thigh under the table. I guide his hand deeper. The older one is in his fifties, still good looking. He makes eyes at Hugh, who hasn't looked at any of us or spoken a single word. Again, Hugh is fantastic in profile.

He's watching us all in the smoky mirror behind the bar. I can't see where he's looking, but I know this. He hates what I'm doing, his own part in it.

They lead us to their room and Hugh gets fellated as I drain one, then the other. No, they're not dead. What do you think I am? They're just unconscious. Spent. Their emotional pocketbooks emptied. Conversely, I'm full now, but still horny.

There are those of us who don't rely on the consumption of flesh to survive. There are those who are preternaturally strong, immune to pathogens, who live on and on, aging ever so gradually without killing a damn thing. Not a single beast, not even a plant. At least, not on purpose. Not usually. I've never cracked open the red heart of a pepper and scooped out its insides. Spicy roots and lacy collars of lettuce have nothing to fear from us. Did you know tomatoes scream? Well, they do. So you tell me, who's the monster?

DAY 2

In the morning, we take long showers, lather up with sweet herbaceous soaps. Our steward knocks and makes offers in a cheerfully apologetic way. I tell him there's no need to ever come back to this room, give him an obscene tip—I do have manners—and send him on his way.

We venture out to tour the ship, passing the "Albatross" brunch buffet in the dining room we've just upgraded to for free, like proper rich people who don't think they should have to pay for anything. Though we're still mid-tier on this ship—the "Sea Dragons" look down at us from the balconies of their suites that cost as much as a luxury car. A sea dragon is a fish that sometimes lances the hands of those unlucky enough to catch it. There in the upper echelon is also where you're most likely to get seasick. We do not get seasick.

We pinch the stems of ornamental glasses filled with tomato and watermelon juices because we like the colors. Then scoot past huge metal trays of mashed-up potatoes with pieces of the skin mixed in, greasy meat logs, and spit-bubble lumps of eggs, steaming and wet. I don't even want to know what the plebian "Herring" buffet looks like.

The antsy passengers are queuing, clutching their plates, craning their necks to see where the line ends, they're so hungry and hungover already. My nose wrinkles at the smell. This is an all-gender cruise, and everyone is wearing everything or nothing: kaftan or speedo, kaftan or topless with nipple piercings. A quiver of top-surgery scars, straight as arrows. Faded yet artful tattoos, impeccable makeup, facial hair, and nose piercings. Hugh is wearing seersucker and a hat and oversized sunglasses. He smells like an English garden. You should always picture him in black and white, by the way. Or sepia.

"You look like you should have a nymph on each arm," I tell him. I imagine him bracketed by dewy waifs. Hmm, a snack.

"Ah, *mi cielo*, but I have a far superior companion." He squeezes my ass like ripe fruit.

I lick his face.

He wipes his cheek with a handkerchief that appears out of nowhere. A gentleman always carries a spit rag. "Count on you to wear Roman sandals to Türkiye." He's looking at my feet.

I'm wearing flat lace-up sandals that crisscross down from my knees over my toes, nails painted opal. I look like a priestess: my dress is a sheath, so thin and soft you can see through to the triangles of white underwear beneath. Bras are just nipple covers to me. We both have skin that appears blessed by the sun, though we usually spend little time out of doors. *We're on vacation!*

"I think that's where we are, anyway." Hugh studied the map on the brochure they sent us in a packet before we got here. There was more information online, which I didn't bother pointing out. Our wristbands might harbor a digital itinerary, but there's no use mentioning that either. He considers Google "cheating," like you're eavesdropping on knowledge. There are multiple sets of antique French encyclopedias stashed in our library, or should I say Hugh's library, since all the books are his. He has a weakness for rare tomes. Hugh's even got a few scrolls that can never be removed from their *capsas*, or they'll turn to sand.

It doesn't matter. We're not home in our skinny house with a poky staircase. Anywhere is somewhere— that sounds like a pseudo-Zen Titter post, or whatever it's called. Hugh went through a Buddhist reading phase and it made him insufferable for at least a decade. It was still better than his origami phase, though, when he filled the house with paper cranes.

There are several ports for the ship to dock at along our way, though we're skipping certain places, and everyone aboard knows why, I'm sure, the same reason this cruise is offering discounts. There's even a page on the cruise line's website about "how to get along with your fellow passengers" that recommends avoiding subjects like politics, including wars and famines. "Our passengers arrive from all over the world to enjoy a first-class, cultured experience. Therefore, other guests may not share your same knowledge or outlook." Then there are columns of "recommended" and "not recommended" topics. Brawls over foreign aid have likely broken out before.

War or no, Hugh and I could disembark anywhere, maybe in Bulgaria or Romania. Set ourselves up in some modest, deserted castle for a few years, live lean, take in the scenery, ensconce like mollusks. But what about our skeletal old house in Cole Valley? It's misty; we're close to the park and The Haight; the streets are home for bands of young hippies, all addicted to painkillers, and their beautiful pit bulls. As Hugh passes by, they fall silent. When I go by, they whistle and the dogs whine and I smile, but I don't meet their eyes. Not my taste. Too lean, too much grit.

We pass pools with swim-up bars and rainbow awnings, including one called the Black Laguna. The water is filtered through charcoal. There are signs warning you not to drink it. And everywhere, there are waiters in white short-sleeved button-downs with gold buttons and cornstarch-white knee-length shorts. They offer frozen margaritas and other slushy drinks squeezed out of a machine, pure-white coladas topped with bleeding-hemorrhoid cherries. Some of the drinks aboard are free, others are not. They also circulate free boiled hot dogs and bread pockets of falafel trailing steamy, meaty smells.

There are rainbow lounge chairs and rainbow bikinis and a rainbow disco with a thatched roof and heart-shaped strobe lights. There's a malt shop called The Harvey Milk Bar. How deliciously insensitive.

I come face-to-face with a digital kiosk advertising a smorgasbord of adult entertainments, plus more sea voyages to sign up for after this one. There are engagement rings for sale with stones big as teeth. "Guess what?" the ad informs us. "They're not just for femmes anymore!" If you buy one, you can get married on your next cruise. Now the kiosk suggests a Stonewall-themed costume party. There's a grainy image of open mouths swallowing wigs. Now it's *Priscilla Queen of the Desert—on ice!* Plus classes: Bulgarian yogurt making, Stalinist flower arranging, plum brandy tasting, Pilates, Morse code. You can ride rainbow waterslides powered by the passengers' own recycled poop. There's a talk on "green cruising," too, even though the poop slide is the only thing that's "green" about this floating behemoth. Oh, well. *We're on vacation!*

To be sure, this ship is a big wet dumpling of lust. Fear, too, though that doesn't interest me. Then there are the desperate, depressed, dependent bodies for Hugh.

I know there are others like us who become cult leaders. But it's a tricky business. You have to fake your own death a lot. Some keep a lower profile, train as therapists, or work at "wellness centers" where they employ ritual spiritual shaming. A certain type, with a less nuanced palate, become funeral directors. Hugh considers that highly uncouth.

We scout a karaoke crowd: theater kids all grown-up in denim overall shorts, tank tops, and open short-sleeved button-downs, drunkenly grimacing their way through breakup songs. Some of them are wearing Mardi Gras beads, others plastic leis. Hugh wanders, sampling the salty, boozy miasma of misery. This isn't quite his taste, he prefers a more existential bite, but they'll do.

Maybe the ship's buffet is better suited to my taste than Hugh's, which is disappointing. Perhaps I should've anticipated that, since we're here to relax after my idiot lover, whose name I've already forgotten—who knows what I am and fed me willingly, perhaps a little too willingly—went a touch mad and burned some of Hugh's things. Some of his art, to be more precise.

My mistake was allowing him to remember where I live. Harbored feelings always fester. Fortunately, the damage to the house is minimal, but Hugh has to find a new studio now. And I could use a new lover.

If only . . . we both think at once. We turn to each other. We are Isis and Osiris, twins who fuck. If only Hugh could form an attachment. Someone tasty yet sophisticated to sustain him through the next two weeks. We smile because now we know what we are hunting for.

DAY 3

By the third night, everyone is feeling at home. There are pita chips in the pools. Groups are forming, pairs are pairing off. Well, really, there is so little time. Why waste it? Fuck now, while you can. And then go rainbow bowling. There's a rainbow ball pit too. There are little speakers hidden all over the ship, and a faggy godmother voice keeps cheerfully welcoming us, urging us to *eat, drink, and play responsibly! And enjoy the free champagne and plum brandy that's clear as water! But don't leave your drink unattended! Or your cruise-issued fanny pack! Or backpack!* This voice I learn, without caring to, belongs to the cruise director, who must have a body somewhere, though I don't know what it looks like. I'd like to find that body and charm it into modulating its voice. Or going mute. Tonight, there's a competition where you shoot cylinders of variously colored jelly into your partner's mouth, with the intention of forming a gelid "rainbow." Winners drink free on their next cruise, if they sign up for it. After that, there's an essential oils event with a guest speaker, *plus discounts and gift bags!*

I dress in something sleek, paint on a smoky eye, slip on thong sandals. Hugh puts on a fresh suit, and we cruise this Albatross bar that's supposed to be a speakeasy with Jazz Age decor.

All eyes are on us. Hugh won't look because he doesn't like it, the attention, the ravenous gaze. I don't look so I can soak up their wanton hunger. I'm wet and sparkling. This is the kind of night where I know I'll draw a crowd—I'm going to drape myself over the piano later. I take a seat at the mirrored bar, but I turn so they can see me in profile. Delicious prickles up my spine. Oh yes. My *bouche* is amused. Who will be the appetizer?

The bartenders are wearing feathered headbands and sleeve garters. The stool I'm perched on is coated in velvet. But a certain damp smell conjures the basement feel of the gay bars of the 1950s, though they were frequently raided by the police, adding a note of danger to the vibe. The biggest risk here is a spilled drink.

A classical butch with rolled-up sleeves and a vest sends over a drink—an old fashioned it's called. Cute. It smells like sweet fuel. The butch nods. I'm thrilled. They're alone, but their friends are here somewhere, they say.

"You should ask them to join us."

Oh yes, they agree, texting without breaking eye contact, they just can't bear to look away. Their friends will certainly want to meet me, too, yes, yes.

Hugh is silent and invisible, a recalcitrant daemon at my side.

The friends arrive. There's a mousy one among them—there's always a mousy one, just as there's always a leader. The mousy one is nervous and fidgety, easily caught. An art student, the others explain because she's too shy to speak for herself. She looks at my toes. I've painted them over, a deep red.

"Oh, an art student," I say. "You must meet my husband, Hugo . . ."

A half step to the left and there he is, in profile, the gentleman himself, like we've just stumbled into an intimate portrait. The others never even saw him. He's impeccable, holding a glass of whisky, neat, which he sniffs now and then like it's an old lover, but never sips.

The mousy art student is transfixed. She knows exactly who he is. Of course she does. Every 101 class features a slide of his photo, *Lilitu,* 1975. Hugh is dressed exactly as he is in the textbooks. And he looks good, he looks very good. No one seems to do the math: in human years, relative to *Lilitu,* Hugh should appear in his eighties. But no one questions why or how a man ages—that's his own business. Whereas I periodically have to make certain adjustments. But never my name. My name I keep.

The old-fashioned butch and friends are silent. They don't know who Hugh is, but they understand something is happening to the mousy one.

"How do you do." Hugh holds out his hand—to shake, or kiss? It's unclear.

The mouse grasps his hand in both of hers. "It's so wonderful to meet you, wow. Wow. I can't believe it." And then she proceeds to tell Hugh about the first time she saw *Lilitu,* his only world-famous piece. The rest of his work is so different, and he's experimented with other mediums, but only the serious Art people know that.

The mouse says she was stricken by it. She couldn't look away. The girl doesn't say "horrified" or "shaken," but you can see it in her face, hear it in her voice.

"I went home and I slept for three days," she says.

Hugh nods. This is quite a common reaction to his work. A certain phenomenon. It's been written about, in fact. As the serious Art people know.

As the girl talks about it, she begins to relive it—her response to *Lilitu.* Her speech sputters to a stop, her face goes slack. She's crying. The grief spreads to her companions and they sniffle. The handsome butch takes a sip of the drink they bought me.

This is where Hugh begins: "I grew up with a lot of opportunities. I grew up with servants. But all around me, people were very poor. There was so much suffering. I was also very alone.

"I went home for a funeral. I began to see things through the eyes of my child self, from the perspective of time, so much time passed, and it was as if my younger self was still inside me, a kernel. I began to take walks, and I took my camera with me. It was dangerous to carry it around. But I took it anyway."

He talks about the things he saw, the maimed dogs and children, the things in the gutter, left in the trash. Babies, body parts. Our circle is somber. They're all looking at the floor, except the art student. I notice the bar is empty, and the music has petered out. The whole room just lost its hard-on. I sigh. There will be no grinding against the lid of a piano for me tonight.

I've heard Hugh tell this story countless times. He always tells it the same way. He never says where he grew up—you're supposed to know. It's implied. So if you don't know, and consider yourself a great admirer of his work, you feel quite stupid. Hugh never says who the funeral is for either. Again, it's implied. Haven't you read his biography? The story is all bullshit, of course. I mean, Hugh might believe it, he's been telling it for so long. He's never attended any funeral, not even to gloat or snack, and though he's taken many walks with a camera, our house in San Francisco is his home. But it's true that the world is poor, and dangerous, and full of pointless suffering.

The art student weeps, and the friends cling to one another like life rafts. How delectable for Hugh. My lover is radiant as a ghost; a visible aura, sheer blue and pulsing.

I vaguely recall a Hugh less burdened by the weight of his soul, assuming he has one. A Hugh who was pleased by my pleasure, however I came by it, and readily took his fill. He wasn't known then. It was before the invitations from universities and galleries, when he didn't need an assistant to manage any of it. His work is too human— it moves them too much. It's too much. Now, when I guzzle all the attention in the room, he looks away.

It's time to call it a night.

On the way back to our room, Hugh keeps surreptitiously touching my ass, gently but insistently. He's satiated, energized, and urgently wants to fuck. I picture myself lying face down on the plush tongue of our pink mollusk bed, naked, legs spread, Hugh's erect cock looming over me. The idea appeals. I am, as always, turned on by the idea of my own body, and the thought of Hugh's dick. But his feast of melancholia has brought me down too. I need a pick-me-up.

And that's when we run smack into Heaven. At first, all I see is *shine*. Then a figure comes into focus, statuesque in a gleaming vintage dress, flowing like there's a fan following them. Around their shoulders, a stole of chestnut curls, shining like Medusa's, before the curse.

"Oh my god, I'm so sorry!"

There's a tiny flower-shaped purse on the ground and a god of some kind standing over it. The hallway light is very bright. A big smile flashes, framed by a dark, perfectly coiffed beard. Cascades of hair. The dress, the silver platform open-toed heels. Oh yes, I think. Oh yes indeed. This is exactly what I need.

Their gaze lands on Hugh, vibrating from his golden

sadness shower, though he's hanging back as usual. He's so gracious, he knows how I like my late-night bites.

Suddenly I'm several feet away, practically against the wall, but I don't remember moving, and in front of me, Hugh and this stranger are leaning in like the close-up in a movie, their faces filling the screen, and the stranger is talking right into Hugh's mouth, and I think they're going to kiss. All their pupils are dilating.

I know Hugh and I know what it looks like when he's in love. Which, until now, has only happened with me.

Then I have the feeling I have seen this person before. Something in their face is so familiar. But I cannot place them.

"Oh my god, I cannot believe I'm meeting you! I am *such* a fan! Do you want to take a selfie?" They look like they're in their early forties but passing for mid-thirties because they have great skin, impeccable style. The flaw is in their voice, which is adolescent. Yet, somehow, it doesn't bother me. Normally, I would grit my teeth—I hate that uptalk bubble bullshit. But I smell sugary vanilla mixed with something strong, something feral. I inhale greedy gulps. Why do I like this smell? Do I always like this smell?

What are you?

Then they look right at me, like they hear me. "Oh my god, I'm so sorry! I'm being *so* super rude. I'm Heaven." An impeccable manicure reaches out for me. Navy-blue sparkles with waves of hot pink. Short, neat squares.

I slip my hand into theirs. The grip is firm, the skin silky soft. Almost like synthetic dick skin. I feel a rush of pleasure, lust. My skin flushes. Oh my god.

"Heaven?"

A well-tended smile, head cocked, hair a waterfall, the light in the passageway casting a halo over uniformly colored roots. Heaven is a stupid name, but it fits somehow, like everything else.

Heaven tells us where their room is, which is higher up than ours, that they're alone, and the room is spacious. They give us their phone number, say we must have drinks. "Drinkies" they call them.

"I absolutely have to talk to you about your work!" they say to Hugh, who beams and blushes. He says nothing.

"We'd be happy to," I cut in, and Hugh nods.

"Amazing!" Heaven whirls off, and Hugh floats like a balloon trailing a ribbon down the passageway, around another, and another, until we reach our stateroom.

"So," I say.

Hugh's still hovering slightly.

"Lie down," I tell him so he'll obey gravity.

He takes off his pants, unbuttons his shirt but leaves it on. His cock is tangled in his underwear. Hugh reaches in and strokes it while he watches me undress. But I know this hard-on isn't for me, and I want to make him suffer for that a little.

I pin Hugh's wrists over his head. Then twist twist

twist. He grimaces but he doesn't say stop. I grind my hips over him, teasing him, then I lean down and bite him until he cries out.

I can share, of course. It's only fair. After all, Hugh shares me nearly every night, an easy feat in our crowded, dirty city.

There was a youth who lived with us for a time, a slim, sensitive creature with rather old-fashioned-looking glasses. Or maybe the glasses were in vogue then . . . I want to say his name was Edgar. Or maybe Igor, or Edvard. He was very much in love with Hugh, I recall. I wonder what ever happened to him. Well, besides getting old and dying. Assorted paramours come and go, our nest of sorrow and lust is here to stay.

Hugh settles into his repose. Meanwhile, I linger. I can't sleep. I'm restless, my hunger unsated. He spoiled my feed. But tomorrow, we hunt anew.

DAY 4

I don't remember Hugh giving Heaven his number, only the other way around, but Heaven texts him the next day. "Hey, what are you two cuties up to today?!" The message is stuffed with emojis, including hearts, unicorns, merpeople, and seashells. On a screen, they're not as charming. I start to wonder if I got carried away yesterday.

I take over the phone and text back, letting Heaven know Hugh doesn't do modern devices. I type out, then delete, a joke about using his phone as a location tracker. I don't want to make him sound like some fuddy-duddy old man. He's old-world, that's different. Sexy. He's a goddamn artistic genius for fuck's sake. We "talk small" for a few minutes about sleeping at sea, the *Titanic*, today's weather, and a TV show about fairies or something that Heaven likes but I've never heard of. Finally, Heaven arrives at their invitation. Dinner, with drinkies, as they say. They've made a reservation already. I like their forwardness. I'm also delighted they've chosen an evening

date: I shine brightest in the dark. And I'm pulling out all
the stops this time.

"Sounds great, can't wait." Message sent.

* * *

Hugh and I spend the day off ship in Istanbul. We walk
and walk amongst throngs of people peering into chic
restaurants serving platters of mezze, clutching cups of
pomegranate seeds in their sweaty fists. We lose ourselves
in a bazaar, two figures in black, with oversized sunglasses,
packed in between case after case of brilliant textiles;
shoes; precious, glittering junk; red hills of spices. We
become invisible to the hawkers shouting in the faces of
some of our fellow passengers, who wear bright T-shirts
and shorts and ship-provided iridescent fanny packs,
with hats.

I see Heaven waving to us.

"Hugh, isn't that . . ." No, it's someone else. They
look nothing like Heaven, I don't know what I was thinking. I guess certain people just have a Heaven-ish sheen
to them.

"Who, *mi amor*?" He seems peckish.

We have to get out of this bazaar. It's too much for
Hugh, and he needs a snack. I grab his hand and elbow-
jab our way through the crowd toward the natural light.
The bazaar contracts, expelling us.

We find a museum full of things so ancient, it makes
us tired. Nobody feels anything in there, it's empty,
they're just seeking refuge from the heat. Why is it so

hot? At home, we don't really have a summer, only disappointed tourists in shorts with chapped knees. The building itself is dark and cool and beautiful. We linger there
for some time, marveling at the tiled dome of the ceiling,
imagining the scaffolding it took to make it. This is the
closest I've ever come to meditation.

We exit and wander the streets. We don't speak, we
just slide our feet over the stones that are older than god,
listening, watching. We don't sweat. We don't pant. We
barely breathe. We don't touch anything, not even each
other, nothing but the crust of the earth under our feet.

Then Hugh jets ahead. He takes a sudden turn into
a narrow stone alley, and I have to run to catch up. I find
him halfway down the block. I don't see anything, but I
hear it: wailing. Hugh's head is tipped back, mouth open.
He's looking up, he can spot where it's coming from, but
I can't. All I see is stone. Even though we know each other's thoughts, in this we are different.

The wailing is full-bodied, an operatic melisma of
agony. On and on it goes, filling the alley. I hang back
to give him room. Hugh closes his eyes, taking it in, the
most exquisite pain. A tiny shard of a tear escapes his eye
and glistens.

In a moment, it's over, the street sounds resume.
Hugh looks at me with love in his eyes. He is full.

We go back to the ship and have sex, slow and steady,
with lots of eye contact. Then we slumber so we will be
fresh for our dinner with Heaven.

* * *

I wear my lips red. A fuchsia cocktail dress, crepe lace at the breast that looks like feathers, bands of velvet ribbing across the bodice. Hugh wears warm chocolate. I don't have to show him what I'm wearing, he just knows. He's overheard there's a bookstore aboard and as we make our way to dinner, he chatters on about it. It's near the spa, next to a meditation room because massage, books, and meditation all lead to slumber. He's very excited. He keeps touching things for no reason: his hair, elevator buttons, gold banisters. Normally, Hugh wouldn't lay a hand on any of this, he doesn't like germs. They can't harm him, but neither can musical theater and he can't stand that either. Right now he has hummingbird energy. He doesn't even care about the bookstore. I wonder if there's an expensive, ten-pound art book in there with Hugh's name in it. His work's probably on a tote, too, or a mousepad.

The restaurant Heaven has chosen is in our "neck of the woods," as Heaven so tactfully put it, since the dining options reserved for Sea Dragons are off-limits to we mere Albatrosses. It's the nicest one we've got, a French-Asian brasserie with colonial touches. The lights are dim enough to flatter almost everyone. The seats are plush. Our waiter is thin and hot and androgynous, and indistinguishable from the others. I flash my wristband—I can't believe I have to wear this hideous thing, plus it chafes—and order a Manhattan because I like the glass it comes in. I like the feel of the stem against my palm, and the dark swirl of the liquor, a black cherry at the bottom, saturated with poison.

Hugh orders red wine because he believes in having wine with dinner, even if you're not eating in the traditional sense. And because Jesus drinks wine. Hugh is such a fan of Jesus, that effeminate anorexic, with his xylophone ribs and over-the-top resurrection, a masochist vamp who volunteers his own blood for others to drink. (Gross.) Inwardly, I sigh. Hugh will always be a fanatic at heart. But that's another thing I enjoy about him. I don't share that kind of passion, but I watch him, and I almost feel it, like remembering a smell.

Our unicorn is late. Making us wait is a power move, on top of our different classes aboard this ship, which I don't care about. But Heaven does, so if I indicate I don't care, it'll seem like I really, really do. I don't like that at all.

The waiter silently delivers our drinks. Then all heads turn at Heaven's arrival. (Oh my god, this ridiculous name!) A few diners snap pictures. Is Heaven famous? Their hair is flowing, dress rippling; they're swimming on air.

"Hiiii! I'm sorry I'm late! I was video chatting with my mom. She is just the cutest!"

Why am I here? More importantly, *how* am I here, seated at a table on a sex barge with someone who talks like this?

Then Heaven slides in next to me and I get a whiff of jasmine and lemongrass and earth. A completely familiar yet new scent, fresh and musty all at once, like they've swapped DNA since yesterday. I want to consume them, belch their perfume. I want to lean into their hair, suck up the lustrous strands like spaghetti. The color is hazelnut not chestnut, I decide, and thick as a show dog's coat.

"How was your day?" Every vowel gets extra time, turning *day* into a three-syllable word. "What did you two do?" *Do* with four *o*'s. I fantasize about wrapping my hands around their neck and squeezing until their hot mouth gapes like a fish and tiny seed-pearl tears squinch out.

"Oh, you know, went ashore, walked around, feasted upon the misery of the living. Then we came back here for a fuck and a nap," I say.

The waiter reappears with a slim flute of champagne I don't recall anyone ordering. Heaven accepts the glass without breaking eye contact with us. Somehow, they are making eye contact with both of us at once. They laugh. Their eyes have a ring of silver around the pupil, the rest of the iris matches their hair. Mesmerizing.

"Oh my god, you are hilarious! Do you do stand-up? Oh, no! Don't tell me. Are you a writer? I know *so* many writers in LA."

LA. Of course. The ditzy cousin to our slightly more intellectual, but still-not-New-York home of San Francisco. I open my mouth to tell Heaven "what I do," as they say, meaning efforts exchanged for money I don't really care about on a practical level, as I do not need money to exert my will. But they turn the spotlight on Hugh, and suddenly I am completely in the dark, like an extra. No, not even an extra. I'm not even on set.

"A writer and an artist. How old New York! Oh my god, I love it. What is this like for youuu, as an artist?"

I've seen interviews like this, where the host aggressively guards the conversation, pretending to let the interviewee speak their mind while force-feeding every word. We don't live in New York! I'm not a writer! I don't even like books! But right now, I do not exist. Heaven has locked eyes on Hugh, and they're both glowing.

Hugh hates questions like these. He hates being put on the spot when he'd prefer binoculars from the shrubbery, so to speak. That is usually how our three-ways with strangers go, anyhow. There's a star, guest star, and supporting. Somehow, Hugh has become the star. This is the problem with unicorns. But Heaven spares him from having to answer because they go right on talking, spouting questions and musings in equal measure. They're telling a story now. I lean in. My gaze doesn't latch. They're not looking at me. They only have eyes for Hugh, who's sporting a pleasurably dazed expression, like an infant drunk on brandy. I direct my body at them, put an elbow on the table, and prop up my teacup breasts. Look at me. Look at me, I will. I exert. My power. Hugh feels it, shifts in his seat slightly, in a way I know means he's sprung an erection. I graze his calf with my toes, shucked from my shoes. Remember me?

"So my chosen name reminds me that there is no hell, that there's only the joy and suffering we create here on earth, in each lifetime," says Heaven.

I have no fucking idea what they're talking about. Hugh doesn't either. He's smiling in his pained way, nodding and watching their lips.

Now they're going on about motivation and self-actualization, not to mention loving yourself, which is not code for masturbation in this case. I imagine stuffing Heaven's pretty mouth with a silk stocking. A dirty one.

"Isn't this place great?" I suppose they mean the restaurant; Heaven looks around. Other guests are watching them and they're pretending not to notice.

"You know there's a secret speakeasy on the ship?" Heaven whispers, and by whisper I mean their voice gets raspy but not the slightest bit quieter. They lean in, and I smell jasmine and lemongrass again. "You have to email a secret account to get a passcode. I went last night." Heaven looks smug, like they know this information is going to make us jealous. Except I don't care about some lame email password. *Email?* Really?

The real brag is all the important people Heaven was with. They drop names, presumably of actors and activists, and someone they identify as the editor in chief of a magazine I've never heard of because I don't read magazines. You'd probably recognize some of them, but it's not even worth the effort it would take to name them.

An inner circle is forming. I'm surprised, frankly, given the ongoing world wars and plagues, that some of these people are here, but surely everyone needs a break? And clearly, we aren't the only ones who got a coupon in the mail. This cruise line has access to a very select mailing list. I'm certain Heaven would love a look at it.

Who then, I wonder, is Heaven? Why were they singled out for an invitation?

Heaven has even more choice information, the creamiest of creams: the inner circle is planning a sex party. All of them are, of course, polyamorous, as I suppose we are as well. Heaven talks like they are in on the planning. It's unclear whether we're invited, or just informed. Frankly, I don't care. I can get an invite to anything I want, if I want. I could make my own sex party if I wanted to. Just watch me.

Abruptly Heaven cries out, "I'm so excited for this cruise!" At that exact moment, the waiter delivers more champagne, again, without being signaled, and Heaven snaps a selfie.

Hugh's lust is palpable, but he's also smiling and squinting in a way that suggests he's found an object worthy of study. A finger twitches, as if to press the shutter. He wishes he had his camera with him. I could slip away, retrieve it from the room, and neither of them would even notice I was gone.

These days, Hugh's been writing poetry. It's a great secret, his agents and other handlers don't know. Opaque and uncomfortable poems that prick you like needles.

He's publishing them in clusters online, under a pseud-
onym. The comments are all cry-face emojis. Perhaps
a book is coming, followed by a book tour across the
country, weeping audiences left raw and befuddled in his
wake. It will take years. We've already established I don't
have that kind of tolerance. But Hugh is infinitely, mys-
tically patient.

"You guys, I really want to take a dance class,"
Heaven says, swilling champagne. Apparently, the ship
has a dance studio offering lessons in hip-hop, Greek
folk dancing, and swing. We do not, as a rule, dance. I've
been known to participate in ritual orgies where gyrating
and swaying are heavily involved, and Hugh may have
writhed under a hooded cloak in an atmosphere of savage
ecstasy, but we don't Charleston or polka.

"Is that what brings you aboard? To find a dance
partner?"

Heaven turns fast to look at me. Too fast, like they've
forgotten I'm there, even though we're all sitting right
on top of each other in the elegantly brassy gloom of
this pseudo opium den. With turtle shells and other
desiccated sea creatures fastened to the walls for reasons
beyond comprehension.

"A dance partner! I love that! That's such a sweet way
of putting it. A partner for every dance, a dance partner
for life!" Heaven waves their hand at me like a hankie.
"Rebekah, you're so cuuuute!"

No one has ever, in the long, varied history of my
existence, referred to me as "cute." I glance around the

restaurant. It's full of eyes, and some of them are on me. My lipstick is a shade darker than my dress, and my petite tits are an amuse-bouche. Then the eyes stray. Heaven is sparkling. My spotlight dims and I feel robbed. What's that expression? Steal the bread from my mouth?

"Actually, I have a partner," Heaven goes on. "Well, I have my primary partners and other committed, ethically non-monogamous partners. And I date. Casually, but ethically. Have you read *Ethical Sluts*?" Their hair slides around their shoulders. I want to seize their flesh with my teeth. With terrible ferocity, I hate and desire them all at once. I could growl. Instead, I grin.

"Are you poly?" Heaven's addressing us both.

Hugh has no idea what they're talking about. He looks at me and shrugs in his elegant way, like a four-teenth-century courtesan.

"In a manner of speaking. We're married." Though the union took place in a temple so old, it's no longer there, and any physical evidence was long ago lost or burnt or eaten by things that like animal skin and tree pulp. We have no license either. What a world, where you need a license from the state to marry, but anyone can own a rare bird or a fish that requires very specific care. Also, children. Anyone can have those, though why they would want them is beyond me. Some humans enjoy suf-fering in a non-sexual context, I suppose. But I digress.

"We're not exclusive," I tell Heaven. I nod at Hugh. He looks surprised to see me, like within the past two seconds he also forgot I was there. I have never been so invisible. I have never been invisible at all, period. I could cry if crying were something I did. Meanwhile, I'm starving.

I take a final shot at Heaven, setting my hand on their shoulder, light as lace. My eyes are so wide and dark—they haven't noticed how unnaturally large my eyes are. They feel they could fall. I trace my fingernail across their cheek, drawing a vein through that glittery film of makeup, and they look at my lips, my soft lips, my lily teeth, my breath like roses. My breasts bloom from my collar, warm and soft with blood. My hair surrounds us, they see only me. I am the only one in the world.

"Oh my god," Heaven says, peering right into my shallow yet enchanting depths at last. I smile. I bear my teeth; I am ready to feast. "Your makeup is so fire. I love your lipstick! Is it Dior?"

I feel like the whole room is laughing at me. I feel weak. These are new and utterly terrible sensations.

Already, Heaven's attention is casually drifting back toward Hugh. I pop off questions, a desperate attempt to keep at least some of the focus on me. "Are you a makeup artist? Where did you study? Where do you get *your* lip rouge?"

"I *was* a professional makeup artist, when I was younger." They preen. "Now, I'm a motivator . . ."

I can't do it, I stop listening. No one needs to hear this.

Their makeup takes on an emerald sheen, like peacock feathers. Heaven's eyes flash with new color. It's beautiful. And strange. I've never seen anything quite like it, and that's saying something.

A glance at Hugh. He's entranced. Nothing matters to him right now.

Quietly, so just the three of us can hear, I say, "What are you?"

Heaven looks at me, aghast, like I just burped in their mouth. "Excuse me?"

"You can tell us. What are you? You're obviously not human." They're no witch either. Witches are everywhere these days and most of them can't perform a single feat of magic. Also, witches smell like shit.

Heaven feigns confusion. "Oh my god, you are *so* funny!" They're not laughing. "Do you know what my friends call me? The last-last unicorn!" Now they giggle-cackle.

I've had enough. "Let's get the check," I say, even though that's not how it works on a cruise ship.

"Oh for sure, for sure. I'm so exhausted. Actually though, before we say goodnight, I heard there might be this informal lecture tomorrow . . ." They name-drop again, only this time Hugh's eyebrows go up and up. "Hugo would loooooove it."

They call him Hugo because that's his name, remember only I call him Hugh. But never mind. It's clear I'm not invited.

I'm done with seduction. I am a furious beast.

But Hugh's thrilled. He doesn't suspect a thing. As a rule—and we have few of them—we don't spoil each other's pleasure. And Heaven's right, I am not interested in listening to some academic talk about . . . well, anything.

"You two should go. I would just be dead weight."

"Oh no, that's not what I said at all! You are more than welcome to come with us!" Their smile is a row of twinkle lights. Hugh's smiling, too, though his lips are still touching. He hasn't said a word this entire time, and he's not even trying to disguise his erection.

"Oh," I say, "I know what you meant. Don't worry. You and I will have a one-on-one after this."

"Oh em gee, of course! That would be so much fun!"

"Yes." I bear my teeth. "It will be."

Game on.

I dream (yes, I have dreams) that I'm in the bathroom at the restaurant that's a tribute to French colonialism in Asia, and I'm standing at the sink, looking at myself. Only my reflection is behind me. I turn to find . . . no one. I turn back and there she is again, looking right through me, futzing with her hair, pulling at her identical waistband, French tucking the exact same loose, sleeveless shantung V-neck blouse. Then the figure's gaze drifts and finally, in the mirror, our eyes meet. The other me winks.

Day 5

The next day, mid-afternoon, Hugh and Heaven attend the impromptu lecture, held somewhere aboard the ship. I don't know or care where exactly, at least at first. Though once Hugh's gone, I worry he'll become entranced, he'll never find his way back. I've made a fatal mistake: right off the bat, you have to establish what your enemy wants most. What does Heaven want with Hugh? Not knowing leaves us vulnerable.

I comb the ship for the most hipster-ish or teacherly among the livestock. I find a group of both having beers by one of the pools, the one shaped like a jelly bean with multicolored glass gumdrops on the bottom and a rainbow waterslide. I wonder if it's the poop slide. Flocks of waiters carefully sidestep chlorinated puddles, holding trays of melting neon drinks.

"Hey, do any of you know where the lecture is with . . . you know, that famous person?"

"What lecture?" says one.

"Oh, with so-and-so?" offers another. I still don't remember the name.

"Yes!"

They give me vague directions with words like *aft* and *stern*. Traveling the ship, I realize, is like moving through an airport in a made-up country. It just keeps going and going, seemingly for no reason, none of the signs make sense. What sadistic Daedalus designed this damn thing? Everywhere, there are little kiosks selling neck pillows and hand towels and bottles of water labeled with the cruise line's logo, a rainbow slapped under it. Plus there's a soundtrack of announcements about safety protocols and *bingo!*

Meanwhile, I think about the best way to learn more about Heaven, which is obviously to fuck them. I mean, it's not like I don't want to. I'm dying to duct-tape their mouth shut and play with their nipples. I don't have to like them to enjoy it. In fact, I might enjoy it even more for *not* liking them. And Hugh would enjoy me enjoying it even more.

I home in on the room, a black box theater framed by stylized portraits of Oscar Wilde, Eleanor Roosevelt, Bessie Smith, and James Baldwin. (Yes, these are names I know.) Is that a velvet backdrop? Is this supposed to be ironic? They all look miserable in their bedazzled state, Baldwin most of all with his big sad eyes.

Muffled by the wall, the lecture has morphed into a monotonous hum, like the sound under sound. I smell psoriasis and sunblock. And I sense Hugh's patient, steadfast attention within. When Hugh and Heaven emerge, I decide, I'll follow them, then reveal myself as if we're meeting by accident. I'll propose we go someplace quiet where they can tell me all about the lecture. Champagne in our room, perhaps? Yes, I decide, this is the move. I check my watch. It's only been five minutes and already I've heard the word *narrative* twice. I look around for someone to flirt with or else this is going to be a long, agonizing wait.

An hour later, I catch up with them (meaning rush ahead then double back) near a sunglass pop-up. These chartreuse octagonal glasses really do look good on me. I slip them into the pocket of my palazzo pants, a pair for Hugh already sheathed in the other pocket, then call out, "Hey, you two! How was the lecture?"

They turn. What a pleasant surprise! What are the odds of running into me here? Heaven is *so* thrilled! Hugh is beaming at Heaven, oblivious to anything else. Everything is peaches.

"I was just doing a little shopping." I slip on the new shades with the sticker still on the lens.

Hugh sees me, takes my hand and covers it with kisses. He is overflowing. I smile. Now I'm aroused. The plan is working. Except I don't want to play with Heaven, I just want Hugh. And a stranger, too, sure, why not. But not Heaven.

Heaven slips past me and coils around Hugh's other

arm. Their tongue whips at his ear. Is the tip forked? They're looking right at me. Heaven is messing with me.

I stick to the plan. "Let's go somewhere quiet and you can tell me all about the lecture. Like our room? Then there's a bed if I fall asleep." I bark a laugh. "We have champagne. And a Juliet balcony." "Balcony" is a stretch—we have a narrow steel plank to stand on, with a railing. Nevertheless, statuesque Heaven would look tiny indeed tumbling head-over-platform-heels into the rabid surf below.

"Oh em gee, you have *got* to come see *my* stateroom! It's, like, the biggest suite on the ship and I didn't even pay for it! I have champagne too. They put pink champagne in my mini fridge! My balcony is e-norm-ous." Heaven grins.

How can we say no? I smile and try to recall which underwear I have on. Feels like a thong.

I try not to be impressed by Heaven's suite, but it's hard. It's dripping in pink, a teenage dream, up at the tippy top of the ship, the smallest layer on the cake, where you can almost feel the waves. If a storm comes, this is the worst place to be. The bedroom is twice the size of ours, and so is the bed. The mini fridge comes up to my hip, not that we need a mini fridge, and it is indeed chock-full of pink champagne.

"Free," Heaven says, preening. Their eyes flash silver.

"Who paid for it?"

Heaven waves their hand like there's a bad smell.

"The cruise line invited me. As an influencer. I'm a brand ambassador for them."

An influencer? Good god. So that's what "motivator" means. Motivate to purchase.

I smile. I'm fairly certain Heaven is a terrible person, or whatever. I move in, take their waist, touch their hair. They smile like this was their plan all along, like they knew I was going to show up after the lecture. I've wandered right into their open jaws, thinking it the entrance to a cave with secrets inside. This kind of threat should be arousing. But with Hugh here, the mood is off. So I perform and pretend.

Hugh assumes his position. He watches. He keeps pulling at his collar.

I'm good, I'm quite convincing. I used to do this professionally—not for the money, of course. For the buffet of want, the eagerness for seduction—and my character still has excellent reviews even though I don't work at that brothel anymore because the people who came there were just too depressing. Sometimes they even cried, and I had to mesmerize them out of it, which ruined the fun. The whole point was to feast upon their irrepressible desire.

Hugh retreats to the closet, peering through the slats in the door. Heaven beckons to him, which is all wrong. I pin their arm back and latch my mouth onto theirs so they can't speak.

But it's no use, the sex doesn't come together, we're performing for an empty room. I don't even bother attempting a feed. I think it's the first time this has happened—who would want to remember?

Afterward, we lounge on Heaven's enormous bed because quickly putting your clothes back on in silence is the only thing worse than a bad fuck. So we're feigning pillow talk. Also, you never know, sometimes there's a second round and things fall into place.

Heaven strokes their own hair like a pet. "So remember the orgy I told you about?"

I do remember, in fact. I'm surprised Heaven is bringing this up right after bad sex.

"Well," their voice drops, like someone might be listening, "it's happening. The whole ship is talking about it."

I wonder how they know what the whole ship is talking about. Do they read minds? How tedious that would be, shifting through someone's thoughts like a dumpster, hunting for a speck of something interesting, a grisly bit about yourself.

Only a handful of passengers will get an invite, though each guest is allowed a plus-one, Heaven tells us. Hugh nods like it's a very interesting story they're telling. Love has rendered him obtuse. If you can call it love. I'm not so sure anymore. I think he might be under a spell, which is worse. Love inevitably runs its course, but spells can last forever. I need to find out what Heaven is so I'll know what they're capable of. Surprisingly, fucking them hasn't been as helpful as I thought.

"I managed to get a plus-two," says Heaven. So smug. Their lipstick is smeared.

We're actually not entirely prepared for an orgy. Hugh didn't even bring his cape. I can't believe we overlooked this eventuality; of course there's an orgy aboard the discount queer Black Sea cruise full of polyamorous influencers.

"All right," I say, like it's no big thing, which it isn't. I pour myself a glass of pink champagne so I can watch the bubbles.

Behind me, there is kissing and fondling and a silky robe slipping open. Then Heaven has Hugh's cock in their mouth, and Hugh is reaching for Heaven's balls. I consider fingering both their assholes. Instead, I hang back and watch. I pretend I'm Hugh. What do I see? I brush my own nipples. This is what I've been waiting for, I realize, as Heaven starts to move like a temple dancer, like a dancer becoming a bird. And then their eyes are green and their hair flashes red, curls coiling fast as snakes. Then snakes strike and fall into long dark strands. Limp, loose curls made of hair once again. Their foot—the nails are growing longer, curling. They could slash Hugh's guts with those things. Then they fall away like pieces of shell, or splintered teeth. Heaven's eyes are closed, they moan unselfconsciously as Hugh takes it long, teasingly slow. They are fully in their bodies, they've forgotten I'm there, they don't even know where they are. And the bed is soft, the sheets are silky in this extremely extravagant room that so effortlessly eclipses ours. I lie back and close my eyes and listen to the soft and wet sounds of their bodies. I toy with my clit a little.

Then Heaven says, "Is this ok?" And I look down at their mouth and nod yes as their fingers and tongue slide around inside me.

I hear Hugh groan. He's watching us, watching me, fucking Heaven hard as they lean over me. He grabs their hair like a harness and pulls. "Uh uh." He's shaking, his muscles are pulsing, the veins pop. He's going to come. I concentrate so I can try to come with him, but in the end, I don't know exactly when it all happens, just that it does and that behind my eyes I watch Heaven take off like a bird with a snake's tail.

We stumble back to our room to sleep like the dead, the kind of slack-jawed sleep you don't fall into in front of a new lover. That is what we have now, a lover.

And I know what they are.

DAY 6

The next morning we have "breakfast" under an umbrella in the sun. I wear my new sunglasses, hair tied up, a few strands loose in the breeze. Sometimes you can actually smell the sea—briny and kind of rancid—like a fog that drifts above the meat smoke, sweat, and cologne. We sit there with nice little plates of croissants and butter, neat white cups of black coffee, miniature glasses of orange juice. I like the colors and shapes of this particular meal.

I know what Heaven is. I saw their true self when they were at their most unselfconscious. I have Hugh to thank for that. But I don't know if he will believe me. Why wouldn't he? I don't know exactly. It's an odd feeling. I'm not used to this, and I don't like it. I am not one to be doubted or disbelieved. Now I must be careful, consider my words like a pauper with a few coins. Somehow, I have lost control of the "narrative."

As if to taunt me, a Heaven look-alike saunters by in shredded navy-blue polka-dotted short-shorts and chunky platforms with a cork heel. They look just like them, and yet, somehow this person is not them. As they draw closer, the similarity disappears and it's just some passenger in something Heaven would never wear. Then I see another look-alike coming from the opposite direction, in orange-cream ankle-length pants and huaraches, with a scarf tied at their neck. Very cute, very fuckable. But again, not the one.

Meanwhile, Hugh is slowly shredding delicate layers of croissant like lace, arranging the shreds into a tower on his plate while surreptitiously keeping a peripheral eye on some skinny, topless lasses with big bushes, shaved heads, and tattoo sleeves.

It's not just that Hugh might not believe me. I have to admit that I don't really know what this revelation means. I imagine Hugh nodding thoughtfully, pretending to sip from an espresso cup. "Is that so?" he might say, and nothing more.

My goal was to identify and assess. So far, I've only managed the first bit.

I also have to admit some of my *feelings* toward Heaven have softened slightly since they stuck their tongue in me. So maybe they're powerful, so what? So maybe they're trying to take Hugh away from me. So what?

What am I saying? I've stumbled upon it: the threat. The only threat there is, really. The only thing I have in this world to lose: my love. My eternal companion. My fellow exile. Without Hugh, what would be the point of any of this?

So I don't say anything that morning under the Slavic sun. I decide to wait until I know more, even though there might not be any more to know. I will at least wait, I decide, until after my one-on-one date with Heaven.

"I'm going to see what Heaven's up to today," I announce.

Hugh's eyebrows surpass the black horizon of his sunglasses. He looks dashing. Devastating. "Ah, *sí*?"

"They owe me a tête-à-tête." I tilt my head and lift my glasses up and down.

"Oh, yes. I'd like to be a fly on the wall," Hugh says, and I laugh. For a second, I think he knows. He's figured it out too. But then I tell myself, no, it's just an expression.

"We'll see."

* * *

For our "grrlzzz date," per Heaven's text, we go to the spa for mani-pedis and massages. It seems like a terrible place to try to get to know someone, with all the silent attendants around. Though silent attendants at a sex party is hot. I have sex parties on the brain now. Maybe silence is the point, I think, nude inside a generous white robe while a pair of women who live on this boat just to scrub our feet silently soak and file my nails and heels. Heaven has an eye mask on and hasn't said a word for several minutes. When they do speak, in a whisper they ask for some cucumber water.

The spa itself appears to have been chunked out of a mountain of black marble. It has a cavernous feel, with honeycomb halls and pool-like alcoves. Everything's moist but also cold. I can't believe the ship doesn't sink from the weight while we lie there, listening to pan flute covers.

It's clear this "grrlzzz date" isn't a date at all. We're just two concubines getting prepped for our warlord to come home and fuck us violently yet unimaginatively from behind. What a boring dynamic Heaven has chosen. What, my attention alone isn't appetizing? They don't find me attractive? Maybe they simply don't like me. I consider this for a moment. I am, in general, quite likable. Irresistible, you might say. Those with reasons to dislike me usually forget those reasons. This is another feeling I'm unaccustomed to.

Well, I don't care if Heaven enjoys me, I decide. I am objectively hot. Therefore we could still hate fuck. What I really don't like is being ignored.

Meanwhile, the ship docks. You can hardly tell. I don't remember where we are, or particularly long to go ashore, but strangers are tickling my feet.

"After this, want to go into port?" I whisper.

"Hm?" Heaven pulls off half the eye mask. "Do I want some port?"

"No, would you like to go into port after this?"

"Ohhhh! Yeah, that sounds so fun. I have to check my schedule, though." They settle back, conversation over. Their schedule, presumably, lives like a djinn inside their phone, and Heaven made a point of announcing when we checked in that they didn't bring their phone, this is their "unplugged" day. Today they're wearing a fabulous kimono-style wrap that sweeps the floor. Somehow, they seem even taller, even without heels.

"We're in Bulgaria, I think. Have you been there?"

"I haven't," Heaven says, with a fake little twist of the voice, like they know they're being curt but they're trying to pretend they're not.

"Aren't you curious?" I say and my hand falls, grazing theirs. I will have them, I think. By the end of the day, they will be under my power, or I will push them into the waves and they will have to join a mermaid collective.

"I'll check my schedule," Heaven says again. Their voice goes flat. They're angry, perhaps. Good, anger leads to mistakes.

"Imagine the treasures we might bring back." I don't say "for Hugh." But I know that's what they're thinking.

"Mmm," they say, sipping cucumber water.

My toes are pink and perky. My nails are filed to points with chevrons of green so dark they look black. I'm ready.

I go back to the room to quickly change, and let Hugh know I'll be gone. But he's not there, so I leave him a note. I wonder, fleetingly, if he's in Heaven's room, if he's actually waiting for them there.

I put on a black dress with a big collar and angular short sleeves, an A-line skirt with an oversized tie at the waist that I shape into triangles. It looks great with my nails. I don my new chartreuse sunglasses and slip into some well-worn black leather sandals that'll be good for walking. As I'm heading out the door, I catch myself in the mirror, pause, and add red lipstick, the shade Heaven asked me about at our "dinner" where no one ordered food.

Then I'm in line, alone among the throng, documents clutched in my sweaty hand, scanning the crowd for Heaven like a lost immigrant. Everyone experiences déjà vu, but have you ever gotten someone else's déjà vu? Anamnesis—that's what happens to me sometimes, like an ancestral or kinship memory gets triggered somehow, some past life thing, akin to an allergic reaction. So I'm standing in line to get off the pleasure cruise and peruse the wares offered up by a Bulgarian port city, and suddenly I'm a traveler, ejected from an overcrowded, stinking ship, rounded up like a traumatized beast. They poke and prod and say things in a language I don't speak. I'm frightened suddenly, standing in this haphazard line, even though the people around me are smiling; they smell like coconuts and aftershave. I force myself to listen in on their chatter. *Yeah, the eggs were pretty good. No, they broke up two years ago. We should check on the kids. Did you check on the kids? I wanna eat a whole crab tonight. What?*

I told you I'm not vegetarian on vacation. The inanity is kind of soothing. I begin to forget the vision, fever dream, whatever these memories are.

Then Heaven appears at my side, and wouldn't you know? It's our turn. But I'm glad they're there.

The water is blue green like crystals. Like crystalline gelatin. I want to be suspended in it. Then, red-tiled roofs resembling rows of cooked lobsters. More stone, ombre layers. Cafés with guardrails so the guests don't fall off the edge into the foamy green surf. We don't speak for a while, we just look, and I can tell Heaven is having the same feeling I am, of wonder and homecoming, like we've stumbled upon an actual paradise. Not because the life is perfect. No, living is pain. But here is beauty, or remnants of it, a reminder of how much there's been, and how much there still could be.

We sit by the ocean with glasses of beer. Heaven drinks theirs first, then mine, without comment. I ask questions: Did you grow up in LA? (No, of course not. No one grows up in LA.) What were your parents like?

"Oh, you know, pretty typical. My mom and I are besties!"

"What's your one impossible dream?" (Humans love this question.)

"Hunny," they say, like it's a joke but also a threat, "I'm gonna change the world."

As they talk, I cross and uncross my legs, brushing their calves each time. I'm fascinated by the garden of their body: legs, crotch, and armpits smooth; swaths of hair across the chest; a short, well-manicured beard framed by their large vintage-starlet sunglasses and flowing hair.

"You have Lady Godiva hair," I say because a compliment is a snack, and sure enough, Heaven eats it up. "Can I touch it?"

They let me stroke their hair. Their hands wander under the table, octopus in a newly discovered shell. The table has no tablecloth, everyone inside can see. I don't care. I'm an exhibitionist, can't you tell? They finger fuck me under the table and the glasses fall off and break and we laugh.

They chase us out of the restaurant so fast, we leave without paying. We are laughing in an alleyway, hanging off each other as if drunk. Well, maybe Heaven is, they've had all that beer. I'm drunk on their rosewood scent—again today, it's different—and I'm not even feeding off them. They finger me while whole families look on in fully aroused horror. The alley is shaded by bright umbrellas in various colors, hanging midair, like magic.

We press each other against the grainy stone walls of the narrow medieval-looking alleyway until we're rolling against the stone with cobwebs in our hair, aggressively kissing and humping. Someone threatens us with a hose.

We fall into an alley within an alley, a stone passageway too narrow for the light to penetrate. Arms braced against the wall, I feel Heaven's cock inside me for the first time, as they heave against me, tongue tracing rings around my throat. I come right away, I can't hold it back. I know that's not realistic, what can I say? Some of us really do orgasm pretty easily. Maybe we just have giant clits and no shame, who knows?

When we emerge, disheveled and shaky, we find the street is dark. There's no inn, no café. The shops are empty, the windows are broken and black. Old men in paper masks scurry by. They don't make eye contact. It feels like the temperature has dropped ten degrees, at least. I shiver. Heaven doesn't seem cold at all, even with their shoulders bare, but they look scared.

"Where are we again?"

"I'm not sure." There's no need to whisper, and yet we do.

Moments later, there's a weird alarm, like a cross between an ice cream truck and a siren. A van with the cruise line's logo on it rolls by, stops. A megaphone pokes out and announces this is no longer an approved location for leisure activities, please get inside the van and reboard the ship.

Heaven and I lock eyes. We don't have to say it, we know what this means: the war has spread again. Like mold over bread. Though some would say that comparison is unfair to the mold, which cannot help being repugnant, just as Death itself can't help being a horror show.

We get in the empty van and immediately our hands clasp. We drive around for over an hour, searching for more passengers, even as we hear gunshots, screams, strangely mechanical howling.

We weigh less and less with each step as we walk the gangplank to reboard the ship, until finally we arrive, weightless. Then we go straight to Heaven's room and fuck for hours until we're soft and loose and spent.

"That was terrifying," Heaven says when we're done. They're lying naked on their back, and I'm on my side, trailing my swamp-dipped nails down their torso.

"It was."

They look at me in a searching, intense sort of way. "I'm so glad you were there with me. You seem like you could handle anything."

I'm surprised, but I shrug, lean in for a soft kiss. "You seem like you can take care of yourself."

"You know, I try to live a life of honesty, with myself and others." They hold their hand over their heart like they're going to recite an oath of allegiance. "I need to admit to you that I misjudged you. I didn't see you. I'm sorry."

"Ok."

"You're really fun!"

I grin, kiss them again, scruff against my skin. I bite their lip. I whisper, "I know."

* * *

It's late, well past dinner. I call the room because I know Hugh will never answer his cell. He likes answering telephones, he likes the *click* they make when you hang up.

"Yes?"

"It's me. I'm with Heaven."

"Oh. Good, good."

"Come meet us for dinner."

"Ah, so it went well, then?"

"You'll see."

This time, it's sushi, Heaven's pick since they're the only one who eats. Though I haven't seen them consume food yet, despite spending the whole day with them. I wonder when and where the fish come aboard, if they load them up dead on beds of bloody ice at the start. I've noticed that everyone chopping, cooking, and cleaning aboard the ship is dark-skinned, probably from poor places that were once rich with resources. I wonder if I'm going to watch Heaven eat out of a shell or slurp up tentacles. The menu—I love menus—features jellyfish and urchins, octopus, giant oysters, raw shrimp smoking on dry ice, decorated with edible but tasteless orchids. Tongues of raw salmon. Stuffed rolls with lobster, even puffer fish, host to a delectable poison that must be removed with surgical precision. I wonder what the food on Heaven's level is like. By now, they must be famished, yet they take the time to change into a fresh outfit. All white this time. A daring choice with so much soy sauce around.

"I'm starving!" they say the moment we sit down.

Hugh smiles. We sit shoulder to shoulder across from him, and his black eyes tick back and forth between us. He's hopeful, but nervous.

"So." He folds his hands atop the table. "How was your day?"

"Oh em gee, I thought we were just getting mani-pedis. You know, like, spa day! But this one is wild. She was like, let's go off the ship, let's smash in public. We got thrown out! I don't even want to know what they were screaming at us, oh my god."

I smile to myself. I actually want to hear this. I'll give Hugh my version later, when we're alone. Right now he's listening to Heaven with the utmost attention, his body eerily still.

"Then something went wrong, and this van came and picked us up and brought us back to the ship."

Hugh's expression shifts. "What went wrong?"

And now Heaven turns to me to explain what we have no words for. "The war." That's all I need to say. I don't even have to specify which one.

Hugh nods, solemn. There are wars in his history. There are wars in all our histories.

"So we went to bed," I add.

Hugh nods, a polite smile. "I assumed."

Heaven goes cute and coy, wiggling their butt in their seat. "I hope it's ok that I kept her away so long," they say to Hugh.

"Of course. Whatever brings you both pleasure." He opens his hands, they fan out and fly away, the body behind them an offering. *At your service.* Hugh the communion wafer.

The waiter brings us martinis with lychees in them, like pickled fruit embryos. Heaven is vegan, they inform us. They order vegetable hand rolls, a cube of tofu in a pool of some kind of sticky sauce, green-and-purple seaweed salad, beautiful in a mucky, alien kind of way. A glance at us, the briefest invitation to try, to sample, but we decline with a slight shake of our heads. Heaven hasn't asked us if we're fasting, or devotees of a diet that eschews most human foods. It's not that they're sensitive, careful not to point out things that might put others on the spot. They just don't care. I respect that. I don't care what most people do either, except as it concerns me, or Hugh.

Meanwhile, Hugh is biding his time, waiting to get to Heaven once we're out of sight. But by dessert, Heaven is yawning.

"You wore me out," they say, flirting but also visibly tired. Their shine is waning.

I feel Hugh's inaudible sigh. I haven't left any crumbs for him.

So when Heaven kisses us each and heads off to bed, I suggest we enjoy the night on our own. His eyebrows sit up like accent marks.

"Wait for me," I say and dash back to the room to change into something that shows off my clavicle. On the way, I pass Heaven in the hall, clad in cerulean. They breeze right by. I stand in the cloud of their perfume.

"Heaven?" I call. But they don't even look back. Another look-alike. Except what if they're all Heaven?

Which means they're not in their room getting ready for bed, they're out on the prowl, same as we are. What is it they're hunting?

I realize then that I haven't once fed off Heaven. Maybe I can't. But what are they leaching from me?

* * *

Hugh and I take a standing table at the back of the karaoke bar. I order martinis for us, and the olives float in glasses that are so cold, they're foggy.

Hugh sings beautifully, like a forgotten god who has swum the ocean of grief. His voice makes everyone wilt and weep. So many of them are here alone. A woman falls from her chair, and no one moves to help her. Hugh feeds, lips apart, an expression of ecstasy or agony.

Then I get up and do a song that brings the crowd back to life, stirs them up a little, something arousing but funny. It doesn't matter if I can sing or not. They scream, dance, shout along, grateful for the boost. "Who is this woman?" they say to one another. "She's hot, I love her!" And I eat it up.

There's Hugh in the back, watching me, loving it. This kind of feeding is ok with him because the audience are willing participants, they came here for this. It's like whoring to him, a fair trade. Maybe I should've become a performer. Hordes of fans desperate to touch you, autographs on the street, stalkers who want to die for you, or kill you. Journalists digging through your trash, every person you encounter filming you . . . No, on second thought, not the right path for someone of my kind. Besides, I enjoy my "work."

I move through the crowd for the finish, and they clap and whoop and reach for me. It feels like sex and sleep all at once, like the warmest pleasure that coats your insides and tickles your bits. It's delicious, it's mana.

Afterward, Hugh and I fall into a dark corner and make out. I feel increasingly as if I am looking back on the present, that each moment has already passed and I am watching myself from the future with great sadness and resignation, urging myself, the me in the now, to savor every fucking moment.

We leave the bar and wind up on an upper deck we're allowed to enter—who cares which one? They're all the same. The ship is loud, its efforts laborious, and the sea churns angrily. Yet somehow a saxophone finds us, jazz carried on the spray. That's where it seems like it's coming from, there's no one around, no bar nearby. It's dark except for the safety lights illuminating the silver banisters, which glisten and wink, beckoning. I want to lean back against the rail, with Hugh's body pressed on mine like heaven against earth, holding me in place, right at the edge. He kisses me and I feel his grimace, he's afraid. He knows what I want and so he does it in one smooth motion. I tilt my head back and he licks my cold throat as I look up at the top tier. Black sugar sky dripping down, studded with little shredded candy stars. Something falls, a dash, like a burst of salt, disappearing into the waves. Then another. They're falling stars, I think. Only I'm upside down, so they fall up, into the water. I rarely notice one, and never so close. Or maybe I have something in my eye. I press back against Hugh, his lips have found my collarbone, but he grinds into me. For a frightening, exhilarating moment, I no longer want to be pressed against the rails, but I'm immobilized until Hugh pulls me upright by the waist. I turn to the water. Invisible, black. What's down there? Did I see something fall? But it's gone.

DAY 7

Tonight is the orgy and I'm bracing myself for disappointment. A boring orgy is a painful affair.

No, fuck that. If things aren't going well tonight, I will make them go well. I will enchant them all if I have to, and Heaven can watch.

The day passes. How we spend it is unimportant, so much so that I don't remember it at all. I'm sure we nap, I'm sure we fuck, at least to pregame. I'm sure we say and do other things. Who cares? Let's get to the orgy.

We're at the door, just the two of us. Heaven may already be inside—we are fashionably late. I'm wearing strappy lingerie under a trench coat. Hugh loosens his collar, unbuttons a button. He's still wearing a jacket.

There's a password to get into the suite stateroom, which Heaven has shared. The Anita Bryant look-alike at the door is surprised we know it. They step aside slowly, with obvious distaste, to let us by. As I pass, I trace my nail up their belly, where the softest parts are, so quickly, so gently, they feel a chill and shudder, not knowing from what.

Then, with a flourish, I remove my trench coat.

"Shoes off," demands Anita.

"Absolutely not."

Hugh takes off his beautiful shoes and the cuffs of his dress pants brush the floor.

"Put your shoes back on," I hiss.

Anita glares, then marches over to a Bettie Page with a silver Indian septum ring to complain about me. Bettie looks at me and nods solemnly. Usually, everyone's friendly at an orgy. These two must be the help. I decide to give them a pass for now, but if they get in my way again, it will end badly for them.

Hugh has taken no notice of Bettie or Anita. He scans the room, then slips his feet back into his lambskin loafers. I know who he's looking for.

I assess the scene. The lights are off, with LED candles and a few candy-red heart-shaped strobe lights. There are open bottles of champagne everywhere, withering rose petals, and people awkwardly humping in the desk chair, others lying on pillows on the floor. The huge flatscreen is set to fireplace mode—more fake fire. I would've put on porn. Four or five people are on the bed, which has been stripped down to the fitted sheet. Strangely mournful music is playing, all vocalization, long vowels, no words, like this is actually a funeral for an orgy. I hear the hot tub going in the bathroom, voices softly laughing, glasses clinking. What's even the theme here? All orgies should have a theme.

I look around for a place to stash my trench coat, and it's at that moment Heaven appears.

"Hi Rebekah!" they whisper like we're not supposed to talk here. Maybe we aren't, maybe this is a silent orgy. Maybe we're all going to get punished. That would explain a lot.

Heaven's wearing a shimmering-green reflective bodysuit that covers them neck to ankles, except for a gap between the legs, where I find silky rayon panties easily slipped aside.

"I'm so glad you two could make it!"

Heaven looks great, and Hugh looks happy. For a moment I think, this is actually going to be quite fun, maybe even quite wonderful.

Then Heaven pulls Hugh aside to "look at something." They'll just be a moment, they tell me, and before I know it the two of them are sitting all conspiratorial on a beige loveseat by the window and whispering, each holding a plastic cup of champagne. I can smell the dry grape fizz. I watch them for a bit, but that's all they do— sit close and talk. Neither so much as flicks the other's nipple.

There's something so obscene about the way they're sitting there talking like a couple on a fantastic first date, while everyone else around them is either fucking dispassionately or watching someone getting dispassionately fucked. It's like they're in some lechers' pit in hell together and have fallen in love, so now they don't mind at all that they're in hell. They're enjoying their own personal hell, in fact. That I'm also here is inconsequential.

So I turn it on, though not all the way up. Things could go too far; I don't need anyone falling unconscious on me. A couple homes in on me immediately. One's got the other on a leash.

"Can I pet your doggy?" I say, and the mistress smiles.

The doggy is fully aroused. They're my first course. I go back for seconds and thirds. I fuck voraciously, acrobatically. The whole vibe shifts. They're all watching me now, as I do cartwheels onto someone's dick. Hugh doesn't notice. I'm feeling feelings I don't care for. Look at me, my love, I plead, fingers and toes splayed. Just a nod to acknowledge this is a mutual experience even though we're apart. That you and I, we are still here together. We are "we." I haven't been abandoned at this lame orgy. I sex surf the crowd, which is like regular crowd surfing, only everyone licks and probes you as you go by. But he doesn't so much as glance my way. His hand is on Heaven's knee. They're vibrating with desire; a forcefield of lust particles surrounds them. No one interrupts. These queers have some manners, and it would be rude to break up their obvious infatuation, like cutting into someone else's birthday cake. There's a dick flopping in my hand, I see. It's made of jelly. Someone is licking me. Actually, someone(s) are licking me. I feel nothing.

I suspect Heaven is holding back so nobody catches sight of any quick semi-transformations. Which means they never expected to fuck in front of everyone here. It also means they probably know that I know what they are, since I was there, I watched them with Hugh.

I fuck on for a while, but I'm too depressed to feed. Eventually people start drifting away. I collect my trench coat. Pieces of my lingerie are missing, and my first thought is someone must've eaten them. My stockings are still on, sort of: they're in shreds. I'll simply buy more. That's all there is to it.

Hugh's still engrossed in whatever Heaven's saying. He doesn't notice my exit.

I find myself alone in our room, already sexed but unsatisfied, which is the worst combination. The cabin is empty and too small. The emptiness overwhelms me, it feels oppressive. The band on my wrist chafes like a manacle. I have to get out of here. I shower quickly, throw on something loose yet elegant, a dash of lipstick, and I'm off. I have no appetite, but I need the hunt.

It's late, and only the drunks and insomniacs are out—easy prey, but unsatisfying ones. Sad karaoke sounds assault me from all sides. The shopping mall is closed, my lithe fingers tick with anticipation. There's a movie theater with late-late-night showings but I don't feel like sitting and being quiet in the dark with no one to look at me.

The sheath I'm wearing chafes my nipples and they

go hard. What a delicious little zing. There, I hear real music now. Fast enough to dance to. Yes, yes. I will rub myself against strangers eager to run their hands under my dress.

The music is sexy and mean. Scary, really. The kind of music snakes would make if snakes made music. The club is very dark, and the only lights are purple blacklights. It smells like alcohol, cologne, spit—human-sex scents. There are just a handful of bodies on the dance floor, a few more watching, half-asleep. There's one bartender in a black T-shirt, back turned to the counter. He looks like arms and a head with no body.

I cross the dance floor. I'm just walking, but I float inside the rhythm.

I wait until they're all looking. Then I reel them in. When there's a mouth at my neck and someone else's hand slipping up my thigh, I decide this is *my* orgy.

"You're so hot," someone says, and I'm very full now, but I won't stop. Not until someone makes me stop, and the bartender sees this kind of shit every night. But I know how to get his attention. I knock a glass over and it shatters. He looks up, our eyes lock.

"Shut the door," I tell him, and he does, then he joins in.

I am full, so very full. I'm laughing and crying, kind of. I feel milk-drunk. What the hell? Might as well go all out. *I'm on vacation!*

DAY 8

By the time I get back to the suite, the sun is up and the room is empty, with shoes and clothes strewn over the floor—all mine. There's no evidence of Hugh at all. Not a whiff.

I want a shower and then a soak, but I don't want to be in the bathroom when Hugh walks in. If he walks in. It occurs to me, for the first time, he actually might not come back.

I don't like how this feels, and I want it to stop.

The door shudders slightly, more of a sigh really, as if answering me. Then it opens.

"I miss keys." Hugh's glowing. He couldn't have slept, but it doesn't show. He glides into the room.

I say things wives say.

"Oh, were you here waiting, *mi cielo*?" His brow ripples. His skin—did they do something to his skin? Hydra oil treatment? Medusa jelly pearls?

"No," I say, and it's true, I just got here.

69

"Oh." He looks confused, like he really cannot imagine why I'm angry, and suddenly I don't really know either. So he was with Heaven all night, so what? I fucked dozens last night, probably. But then I think about Heaven and Hugh whispering and sitting so close without really touching, the two of them alone in a room full of people. And me. I used to be the only one in the room.

"What are you doing with Heaven?"

Hugh seems surprised, then pained. He doesn't say anything for a while, and I can't tell what he's thinking. I want to scream but I don't.

"I don't know," he says finally.

"I don't feel like I'm a part of this."

"Well," he's talking so slowly, every syllable trembles. "I wasn't part of things with . . ." and he names the ex-lover who lit his art on fire.

"What about . . . What's his name? Who lived with us? Or the couple across the street, remember them? I had them sell their house?"

"Yes, my dear. I remember."

"So I owe you this?"

"No." Hugh shakes his head. His hair looks longer.

"What if I want it to stop?"

He shrugs the way a dancer would shrug. How beautifully he creeps about, my love, sighing and shrugging. Metal spikes in my chest—that is the feeling, it's medieval.

"What if?" he says, which means, *don't ask this of me.*

"Ah." He clears his throat. "In fact, I was going to propose a day with Heaven, the two of us. I'd like more time with them."

I am shocked. "*More* time?"

"Rebekah . . ."

"That's fine. It's only a short trip, by all means, my love. Explore. Wander. Get lost." Jealousy is the most unpleasant emotion. It tastes bitter and you can't ever scrape it off your palate.

He gives me a pitying, soft-dick look. Oh no, this will not stand. I do not like the flavor of pity either.

"I'm going ashore." I make the decision as the words come out.

He's surprised for a moment, then smiles and nods like a concierge. "Do you have your passport?"

What is he talking about? I'm the one who carries the documents, who pays the electric bill. I want to throw him against the wall and remind him who I am but I'm too irritated to play. Also, I'm worn out from my escapades.

"Of course I do. I'm the one who carries yours, remember?" I slink into the bathroom to shower.

When I come back out, all clean and moisturized, he's already gone.

* * *

We're on Romania's rim, docked at the port city of Constanţa. It's hot here too. There's a small castle-like structure on the shore, and the shore itself is just rock.

The rock rises into craggy cliffs, worn and wormy from sea and salt, where even birds can't find purchase. *Eau de Nil*—that's the color of the water, from the beautifully blooming algae. It's likely infested with thirsty sirens— somewhere in this country there's a famous mermaid statue. Maybe I'll see it today. I don't know where it is.

There are signs for a casino. A casino? Streams of people are following the signs, even though there's a casino on the ship. I don't have a plan, so I trail the crowd, just to see where they go.

It's actually a palace—the European kind, ornate and the color of old bone. It's a corpse, this building, with scaffolding sticking out like exposed ribs. The tourists swarm, taking photos.

I slip into an alleyway, which is full of street cats who narrow their goopy eyes at me and hiss. I hate cats. I mean, normally, I don't really care one way or another but today, I hate them. They can tell. A greasy black one with yellow eyes growls and swipes at my bare ankle as I go by. I whip around and a curse escapes my lips in a tongue I don't currently speak, another conjured memory from a time long ago, like that immigrant's memory from my first trip off ship. What is happening to me?

I've never thought much about "who I am" or "where I come from." Blech, so cliché. Besides, I've always had this tacit sense of my history, like a beautiful poem in another language that you know by heart, even if you've forgotten what it means. Only now, I come to find I don't remember the sound of the words either.

I wander around, pissed off, not paying much attention to where I'm going. I trample through some ruins, then someone's garden. An old witch curses and throws a shoe at me. I move faster. I pass cafés with tables outside, umbrellas and red folding chairs. People eating and talking in sunglasses. Pouring glass bottles of mineral water into glass cups.

Then I find the mosque. It's a Byzantine fairy tale of a building with a crescent moon on top like a goddess's scepter. It seems completely out of place, a mirage. And yet it also could not possibly exist anywhere else. I'm nervous for some reason, but the mosque is open to me, so I go inside. And all I see is blue. Intricate domes of blue, the giant eye of the god I don't believe in. It is all so wonderfully ornate. I feel dizzy. I don't really recall ever feeling dizzy before. It's not entirely unpleasant. I would lie on the floor, but there are tourists milling around, mouths agape, bumping into each other like sleepy flies. I am a tourist, too, I know. But it's different because they smell like yeast, and they clump together in awkward formations. I am alone, svelte as a sickle. I slip past them unseen.

I am by myself in a new way here, as if I am a small thing. I've never thought of myself this way. I feel like I'm falling. Is this, I wonder, a religious experience? The temple ignites. The flames are blinding, my flesh melts and I scream.

Everyone is looking at me. Fuck, I've just had another déjà vu.

Where was I born? It's such a simple thing, so simple there's no need to ask. Except I don't have an answer. I don't know. Maybe I'm rooted in this place, maybe I'm getting closer to something.

I want to go to the beach. I want to lie in the sand naked. I didn't bring a bathing suit anyway. Maybe there's a nude beach.

When I exit the mosque, I listen for the ocean, follow the direction of the breeze. I walk so very far, but my feet never tire. If I get lost, I can scale the tallest building, look for the ship to lead me back.

Hugh is with Heaven somewhere right now, probably in bed. Talking in bed. I can't picture them doing anything but talking now, like that's their kink, only they're also naked in my mind. At least I can fix that part. I add a pimple to Heaven's ass.

The wind off the sea whips my hair and lashes my face until my eyes tear. It feels like my eyes are bleeding down my face.

A man stops me and asks me if I'm all right. I know that's what he says even though I don't speak his language. His hand grips my shoulder, hard. This man will do me harm. His desire is rotten, fetid. I give him a little shove and, for a moment, he's airborne. And then he's moaning on the ground, paralyzed, perhaps. It's really just a push, he just doesn't see it coming. But he deserves it.

* * *

The sea is big and rough and loud. In line to get back on the ship, there's nothing to do but stare while struggling to fend off the chatter on all sides, until I give up. So I listen for something at least halfway interesting. I'm quickly disappointed.

Then someone behind me says she saw so-and-so on board, and by the way she says the name, I know it's a celebrity.

"No way," replies the friend. "It must've been someone who just looks like them."

She swears it really was what's-their-name.

"But it doesn't make sense. What would they be doing on this cruise? They're not performing or anything. They probably have their own ship."

"Maybe they're the spokesperson!"

"But they're not in any of the ads."

"Maybe it's a new contract and they offered a free cruise."

"Yeah . . ."

It's plausible, but I agree, it seems unlikely.

I realize it must be Heaven they saw. Heaven impersonating someone else, someone other people would undoubtedly recognize. Maybe that's who their suite is actually reserved for. They like pretty things—who doesn't? They like attention—ditto. Maybe Heaven desires more, the most; they court worship.

It's hot. The line isn't moving. What are we waiting

for? I don't understand why every human thing takes *so long*. So much time is just pissed away by the same people with so precious little of it.

When I step aboard, I feel a rush of relief, until I realize I still have no idea where Hugh is. I race back to the room and, of course, he isn't there.

I lie around and get off while I wait for him. I hate that I'm waiting for him. It's boring and cliché. I also can't believe I didn't bring more toys with me.

When he comes back, he seems very happy and also extra somehow, fluffed up. He's got a soft, well-moisturized glow, perhaps from a facial with baby snail goop or something.

"*Mi amor.*" He beams.

"Did you hunt?"

"Oh. No, I forgot." Hugh slips off his jacket.

He didn't forget. "Did you?"

"I guess I didn't need to."

They're giving him everything he needs. They're his *cielo*. I take Hugh in my arms and kiss him. He tastes like frosting, the scent of this very expensive lipstick Heaven wears, which is probably "designer." They probably can't afford it, they pretend to be other people to get free stuff, too, I bet. I can't fault them, that's what I would do.

When he starts kissing and rubbing against me, I'm surprised. But also pleased. Then he throws me on the bed. Delightful! I actually fly through the air. This is new, this power, this confidence. It's them, I realize. It's

Heaven's influence. Well, maybe this will work out after all . . . I cling to him as he rolls me around and I close my eyes, tumbling blind.

DAY 9

Hugh's sleeping face wears a petite smile, and a little drool. He seems so content. I'm waiting for him to wake up and tell me about his day with Heaven, and I've been waiting a long time. Hugh never sleeps this late.

When he finally opens his eyes, he pulls me on top of him. He burrows in me, smothers himself with my body. Then he pulls me into the shower. Afterward, we go sit outside at a table set for breakfast, though it's practically lunch now, not that it matters. Hugh keeps smiling at me, touching me. But he doesn't say a thing.

"Where are we today?" This could mean several things, I realize, as the words come out.

"I don't know actually." Hugh smiles.

"What do you want to do?"

"Oh, I don't know, really, *mi amor*. I thought I'd compose some poems."

This conversation is so mundane. I'm bored.

There's a handmade postcard stuck to my shoe. It's a picture of a backpacker on a trail, smiling and kneeling

79

next to a wiry little dog. This person is missing, apparently. The postcard makes no sense to me. Why this photo? Did they disappear while hiking? What does that have to do with the *Zorya*? Is the dog missing too? I imagine someone got too drunk and fell asleep in an odd place. Their friends made the flier as a joke. You can't disappear when you're trapped on a ship. Unless, of course, you fall overboard. I recall the stars like salt sprinkles falling over the upper deck. They looked so beautiful, so unreal. It was my imagination.

As if on cue, the cruise director's disembodied yet chipper voice reminds us all not to leave personal items unattended, there are lockers by the pools if we need one, and to exercise caution when drinking aboard, especially at night.

"We need to talk about Heaven."

Hugh jerks, just once, like there are strings attached. He picks up his water, looks down into it, puts the glass back. "Oh?"

"Yes, my love."

Hugh nods. He's panicking, I feel it, but on the outside, he doesn't move. "I'm . . ." he begins, falters. Clears his throat, tries again. "I'm still processing the experience."

Processing? This is Heaven's language. "What experience?" I want Hugh to say it.

"My day. With Heaven. It was . . ."

"What?"

Hugh holds up his empty hands, as if they're supposed to be full of words. He's at a loss.

I dig my nails into my palms. "Ok, so you're in love with them . . ."

We don't put that much stock in love, but I don't know what other language to use. *Infatuated. Bewitched.*

"Well, yes. It's like I'm someone else . . . I feel the way someone else would feel, and I don't need the refuse of human emotion, this bottom feeding . . . In fact, I've lost my taste for it."

"Bottom feeding?"

He blinks, realizing what he's said. "I don't mean . . ." But he does mean, and he cannot recover, he isn't quick enough. "They're never sorrowful, I mean. I've never experienced anything like it."

I'm actually frightened. I do not recognize the shine in his eyes, little drops of oil. It's not just love, or desire. It's greed.

I don't want to hear any more. Suddenly I'm standing.

"The sun is too much. I'm going to lie down for a bit."

Hugh nods. "Well then. Rest well, my dear."

I lean down, kiss his cheek, and walk away. His eyes don't follow. He'll go off somewhere to write his poems he won't show me. Or maybe he'll stay right there, until the waiters work up the courage to ask him to please leave, sir, so they can clear the table.

Meanwhile, I head straight to Heaven's suite.

* * *

I knock three times but there's no answer. There's music and glass clinking. I can smell their perfume—it's fresh.

"It's Rebekah," I shout, pressing the doorbell.

There are a lot of scrambling and scratching sounds, and then the door opens. They're in a white T-shirt and robe, no makeup, but they look dewy and coiffed. Their hair is shiny and silky. They've straightened it, I see.

"Your hair looks nice."

"Hi! Oh, thank you! Do you wanna come in?"

"Yes." There are personal items all over, a portion of which Heaven is bound to forget later: compacts, accessories, various gift bags and tufts of tissue paper. I smell vanilla and sugar—there are baked goods somewhere, out of sight.

"I'm so glad you're here, communication is so important, and I'm so excited to catch up with you." Heaven talks like all their thoughts are scripted. They sit on the plush sofa big enough for five and pat the cushion beside them. Their toes are a different color than they were the other day. Did they get another pedicure?

"What do you think I'm here to communicate about?"

"Oh, hunny." Sad face. "I'm sorry, we can talk about anything you want. You tell me, okay? You start."

I find their mock pity repugnant. And suddenly I don't know what I came here to say. What do I expect from Heaven? I want them to explain what's happening to Hugh, I realize with horror. How humiliating, to have to ask *them*.

"Can you only do animals?" I already know the answer.

Heaven doesn't miss a beat. "Humans are animals."

"That's what I'm asking, can you do humans?"

They cock their head, and their face shifts oh so subtly. It's them, but not quite, like they're their own sibling, like one of the many look-alikes I've spotted.

"So who's the real you?"

Heaven beams. "I'm always the real me."

"But is this really what you look like?"

"What do you really look like, Rebekah?" They say my name hard, as if they don't believe it really belongs to me.

"I don't have any control over my appearance."

They cock their head, and their eyes flash yellow, which, I have to admit, is pretty cool. "You do, though, don't you? I mean, doesn't everyone?"

Eye roll. "Ok, fine. Everyone is a metaphoric shape-shifter, everything is costuming and illusion. There is no reality, everything is interconnected, I get it."

Exaggerated sad face, like I don't get them and they do *not* love that for me. This must be what seasickness is like.

"If the ship sinks, would you turn into a whale and save us?"

"Are you seriously asking me that?"

"Are dolphins whales?"

"I don't know. They're mammals, though."

"That's true." I nod. "What about a giant sea turtle? Or a salmon?" Salmon live in the ocean, too, right?

Heaven purses their lips. Knowing selfie face with I-mean-business eyebrows. "We're not going to sink. Don't manifest shit like that, girl."

"Of course not." I'm unconvinced because I'm already sinking. "We won't sink."

"So is this what you came to talk to me about, hunny?" Heaven gives me sympathetic sad face now, like they're the life coach and I'm the schmuck stupid enough to sign on for this reality show.

Underneath, I sense their unrepentant, insatiable desire. Whatever I've got, they want it. They're going to suck me clean, like the oysters they claim not to eat. I can't help it, it kind of turns me on. But not in a good way.

Heaven doesn't want to know me, they want to consume me, and in doing so, absorb my potency. They probably have a whole collection, like handbags. It's so clear to me now. How did I not see it immediately? But I know the answer. They blinded me with silk and lipstick, that grating uptalk. They cloak themself in dumb beauty.

"Have you ever turned into something predatory? Does the hunter's instinct kick in, or do you still feel like you?" I want to know if Heaven has ever torn a body apart.

Heaven gives me a look like "who would think such a thing, what is wrong with you?" I'm not buying it. I'm convinced the answer is yes, they know what a mouthful of blood tastes like.

"I'm not a werewolf." But their laugh is a bark. Was that on purpose? In any case, they sound angry. How dare I?! Oh yes, I dare. I am very daring.

"I'm closer to a god than I am a monster," Heaven adds quietly, with the haughty tone of a monarch who mutters to themself while the handmaids pretend not to hear.

The word *god* shocks me just a bit. I've already figured out they bask in adoration. But it's a whole other thing to hear them talk about divinity. Even I don't stretch that far.

I decide to pretend they didn't just say that. "But could you be one, if you wanted to? What about a dragon, or a chimera? Could you turn into a sphynx?"

Heaven eyes me coldly, frowning in a way that will lead to wrinkles. Their face is transformed, minus the smile. The eyes are dead. Oh yes, here we go. I want to see the real them. Bring it, Heaven, reveal yourself to me.

"C'mon. Turn into a puppy. One of those ugly-cute ones."

"You're being really insensitive."

"I don't think I am."

Heaven has great posture, but somehow they're stretching even taller now, so I have to tip my head back to keep my eyes on their face. It's official-official: I hate Heaven. My hatred is thick and cold.

They square their shoulders. Their eyes are green yellow. Chartreuse, a color named by grumpy Carthusian monks trying to mix up the elixir of life. I don't know how I know this, but I do. I've absorbed many things over the years. And now, after all this time, I know a shapeshifter. The first I have ever met, I think. How strange this life is sometimes.

"You're not really a vegan, are you?" I smile. Heaven is a carnivore if ever there was one.

Their yellow eyes go wide. Their lip curls. Is their facial hair thickening? I never noticed how long their ears are . . . Nope, it's happening. They're changing right in front of me. They can't help it, it's the rage. I recognize that I should be afraid, but I'm fascinated. I also haven't engaged in combat in a long time. Heaven will test my mettle.

Heaven bursts out laughing. Their posture collapses, their shoulders slink down, and they toss their beautiful hair like they're in a shampoo commercial. Then they comb through it with beringed fingers and give me *that* look. Ah, they're going to sex-glamour and seduce me. All right. I lean in, press my breasts against them. I like sex with someone you don't trust. It's thrilling, not just the hate fucking, but the rush from the risk: you might get fucked *and* stabbed. I'm immediately wet.

My hands aren't clean, only my mouth is clean. Heaven claws, I claw back. They hiss, I roar. Their hair stands on end, a halo of brown silk. I've never seen anything like it.

We fuck out all the things we can't say, or do, like destroy one another. The pain is exquisite.

Then it's done and we look wrecked.

"Let's go somewhere and tell them we got robbed," I say. Pity isn't my thing, but what the hell, why not try something new for a laugh?

Heaven looks like they need a cigarette, though I haven't seen them smoke. "That's kinda psychotic."

I shrug. "How many people live in your house in LA?"

Heaven resumes combing out their luxurious hair. "What do you mean?" They're stalling.

"How many do you have?"

"How many what?"

"Fine, don't tell me." That means it's a lot.

I suspect Heaven is a small-time cult leader. Are only some of their horde for sex? Do they wait on Heaven hand and foot? Who needs a vacation in that case? Unless of course . . . Yes, they're here looking for fresh victims, who come from faraway places where no one will ever figure out what happens to them. With Hugh's powers, his minor fame, he is an excellent catch. Suck me dry, take him home—that's the plan.

I would like to get off this ship. I would like to fly fast over land, through the trees. I would like to claw the dirt and observe the gibbous moon crowning the hillside. Some primal tie tugs at me.

I quickly reassemble myself and move for the door. Heaven follows. They grab me and grip my hip hard, pressing an already healing bruise with their thumb. They kiss my cheek. Their beard is rough.

"Give Hugo my love." Hot breath on my face. Burnt honey. "I'll see you both soon." Chills.

"Not if I don't see you first." I laugh, pointing finger guns at them like it's all a great joke, they're not my enemy at all, not at all. *Pew pew!* I laugh. We lock eyes. I smile bigger so I can show off my teeth.

* * *

When I open the door to our room, it's like Heaven has just been there, I just missed them, their bouquet is still swirling in the air. Now it's peonies. How? How do they do it? Did they turn into a fly and zip over here? Can a fly wear perfume?

Hugh doesn't look up, and I think for a moment he knows I just fucked Heaven, they were here a moment ago and told him, and for some reason that's a problem, he's getting possessive.

He's sitting on the edge of the ridiculous bed with his elbows on his knees, fingertips touching their twins. "I've been thinking," he says. No hello, no kiss. And still, he doesn't look at me.

I'm too late.

"I've been thinking," he says again, forcing the words out. Then he takes a deep breath.

"I don't want to hurt you." Hugh exhales and his voice cracks at the end and a piece of my heart likewise chips off. "I feel things with Heaven I've never experienced before. Things I didn't even know were possible." He takes another deep breath, gulping the air like a drowning man. Did you know, if the water is cold enough, you take a deep, involuntary breath as soon as you go under? And then you're sunk. Again, I don't know how I know this. And yet all I see are dead bodies bobbing among ice floes.

There, he's said it. Hugh sits there in an elegant hunch like a Rossetti painting, with that exaggerated brow and chin, still not looking at me.

But when? I want to know. When did this happen? I just saw Heaven, my mouth was just on theirs, I have their fingerprints in my flesh. Not enough time has passed, too few scenes have gone by, we are not yet far along enough in the story for this. It's too soon, I want to say. I still have time. As if I'm still in *my* story, the one where I'm figuring things out, I'm the protagonist, and not, in fact, in Hugh's story. Where this is about him, and Heaven, too, and not about me at all.

"You're leaving me."

He won't look at me, damn him. He takes such a long time to answer, and meanwhile I am caught in this waiting like a wave. I can't resist it; I just have to ride it out.

When Hugh finally speaks, he says something I can't even comprehend or remember because it isn't a reply, so I don't bother recording it. It's nonsense. Which means yes, he is going to leave me.

Then Hugh says, "Heaven understands this world in a way I never have."

I am frightened. Truly frightened.

"Their perspective is entirely fresh. It's like being young and new again."

I'm his old life. Fuddy-duddy wife. He doesn't need me anymore. And if I strangle his lover, slit their throat? Hugh will mourn. He'll be inconsolable, he'll make up fantasies of what might have been. Worse, he'll turn it into Art.

"Heaven has ideas, plans." They have thoughts about collaborations, interactive installations. All Hugh has to do is call his handlers, who didn't want him to go on this trip, I remember now. Their disapproval seems prescient.

"Heaven," he begins slowly, knowing how ridiculous this sounds, "believes we live many lives, have many selves."

"Yes, of course they believe that." If you live forever, you don't reincarnate, now do you? You can reinvent yourself, though.

"Please, *mi amor*." He's slow, so patient. "Please let me finish."

So I do. I let him finish. I move not a muscle as Hugh explains Heaven's theory of the meaning of existence. My body burns cold, then hot, then cold again. Then I leave my body for a moment. It's still there, but it feels dead. I sense the weight of it. What if I opened the door to the balcony and blew away like a spider parachuting silk?

"I feel . . . confined by this life. I cannot help but wonder now, what am I missing? This idea obsesses me."

I am stunned. All these years, we've lived in the same familiar city that he loves, where he can walk and walk, up and down the hills, without looking where he's going because he always knows his way home. We occupy a decaying old house that was once purple but now looks gray, with lush starbursts of green overtaking the front steps and the zigzagging banisters. Tourists emerge daily from the mists to take pictures. Every floor inside is slanted, and the stairs are narrow and too high. We live there because Hugh feels at home there. I would just as soon live in New York, or Paris. Fuck me, even Vegas, just for a change. Now that might be fun.

Fun. We're supposedly here to have fun, just like everyone else. *We're on vacation!* Catharsis, a rendering, is not "fun." Hugh has caught a fever—vacation fever, a disease borne of confinement and too much pleasure. He's hallucinating.

"Don't you see?" he says. "Every human is a delight, a succulent flower, plush with feeling. Every single one has something to give. Every single one is dessert. Divine dessert. I can be better than what I was. For the first time, I want to be better. Heaven has promised me I can. Heaven is more evolved than we. Heaven has seen the way."

I'm suddenly so exhausted, I can't even roll my eyes. It doesn't matter anymore whether Hugh actually knows what Heaven is, because he believes that he does. There are no secrets between them, he thinks. If I tell him right now they're going to enslave him, chain him to their LA lifestyle, he'll smile. Fucking masochist. He's always harbored Catholic tendencies.

Hugh doesn't want to be what we are. And Heaven has promised him he doesn't have to be anymore, that he can transform into . . . what?

No, not what *we* are. He doesn't want to be what *I* am. He's felt this way for quite some time.

I fucking love myself. I have never wanted to be anything more than what I am. To try, for Hugh's sake, would be false. Who would I be then? Time passes, wind or water over stone. The stone is the stone. Hugh knows this about me as well. He's seen me crouched naked over the prey I've rendered unconscious with my lusciousness. Their heads loll and their eyes roll back, and I grow full. He's watched me feast, and it repulses him. He repulses himself. He sees the thing that disgusts him in me, and my pleasure in it is a reminder of what he is.

I realize what fascinates Hugh about Heaven is exactly what he once found captivating about me: they're self-centered, yet attentive, and living by an utterly selfish credo. Heaven is unabashed in their self-love, rife with secrets, ever ready with a promise, especially to keep a lover.

Have I kept him like a pet all this time? Did I deceive Hugh? Or did he deceive me? Maybe he never loved me at all, for lack of a better cliché. The thought makes me fall inside, like I'm dropping fast through the dark, but I haven't moved. Maybe he isn't my twin.

"All I've ever wanted is your happiness," I say, and Hugh winces. I don't care if he believes me. I'm selfish, sure, but as much as I'm capable, I have put him first.

"Follow your pleasure, my darling," I say, and kiss him, with tongue. A little flick, and gone. If only I could evaporate and crawl like fog over the sea. What a perfect exit that would make. Instead, I have to walk this flesh from the room, so I do it with my shoulders down, leading with my hips. I force myself to go slowly. I feel his eyes on my back.

But where am I going to go? Right, he will go to Heaven's room. And I can stay here, once he's cleared out. And then we'll all get off this boat again, in a different formation: still two against one. Fuck that.

Where's the next port? Where are we headed? I can disembark anywhere, adopt a new identity, disappear.

I wander the ship. Smiling people rush by, people in inflatable unicorn donuts, carrying all manner of things. I think I spot the couple from the first night, but I'm not sure, I can't quite remember their faces. For a moment, I'm stricken. What if that one is actually Heaven? Or that one? I sniff the air—nothing unusual. I check all their shoes. No, Heaven wouldn't wear any of that.

I stand at the railing and look down. I'd have to climb up high, then jump way out in order to clear the side of the ship. I wonder what would happen to me, if I would drown. Can I drown? Would something swallow me? These are questions Hugh wants answers to. He wants his existence to have a meaning beyond pleasure. Beyond me. Something is physically happening to my heart. This pain, it's spreading all over. I feel like I am dying. What now, what now? I could do anything, go anywhere. The thought is exhausting, terrifying. What's the point, without Hugh?

Maybe neither of us will return to the house when this is over. It's full of things. I can get new things.

I go find a washroom and fix myself up. Then I hunt.

* * *

I'm fully dressed in a cabin with three naked people who are laughing like they're high. They're high on me. Their eyes are shiny, and they forget to blink. But the giddier they get, the worse I feel, which isn't how this is supposed to work. I can't even feed properly now; I've lost my appetite.

These quarters are mine now, and yet they're full of these other people's things. The things I don't like, I tell them to toss overboard from the balcony, and off flies a flamingo scarf. A canister of spray-on body glitter drops like a stone. Then, from the sole chair in the room, I direct them: fondle this, lick that. They do everything I say but they don't do it to my liking. I tell them to smack each other across the face.

"Yes, mistress." *Crack*! Their eyes tear.

"Look at me."

They stop, gape.

"Tell me what I look like to you."

"You are so beautiful." Their pupils are dilated. They're drooling a little.

"You're sleek, like a panther."

"And sexy."

"So sexy."

"Classy too."

"Yes."

"Do you love me?"

"Yes, oh yes. We love you."

"I love you."

"I do too."

"Put your clothes on." I go to the bathroom and close the door, splash water on my face.

When I come out, they're wearing each other's clothes in the wrong order, on the wrong parts. It takes several minutes to sort it all out. I'm coming on too strong, I'm going to hurt one of them. Well, at least one, but I don't really care. Hugh doesn't want to be a monster like me? Fine, I'll be the monster. I'll be a greater monster than

Heaven, even. Hugh will have no choice but to bow to my magnificence.

I send forth my minions to collect my clothes and toiletries from the suite. I know they're not up to the task—that's the point. I want them to ruffle Hugh a little, remind him what I am—what he is. We are the most highly evolved of parasites. We feed, then we make you forget. We don't do it out of mercy, we do it because it works. Because this is our nature. "Embrace your nature," I say by sending my human sex dolls to retrieve my shit.

They return looking bedraggled, my suitcase in tow. When I open the bag, I see and smell his hands on it all: he's carefully packed all my things, my passport right there on top. It's like I've been struck. I fall back, even. I must seem overcome, or dead, because the minions shriek.

"Shh, shh, it's all right." I tell them to order champagne. I enjoy watching them drink it straight from the bottle, bubbles spilling down their chests. They are children again in the garden, probing each other with sticky little fingers.

I summon them to me. Like demented handmaids they remove my clothes. They're clumsy, their nails scrape and scratch. I don't mind. They beg to pleasure me, and I lie prone and let them. Sometimes my eyes are closed, sometimes open.

I imagine traveling home with them, wherever that is. I could check their IDs, look through the pictures on their phones to find out. Perhaps they live in a nice, cozy house. I could stay there as their guest; they would provide everything I need. I could travel the world this way.

I tell them to stop, leave me alone. I want to rest now. They can sleep on the couch like pampered dogs.

* * *

They're still sleeping when I get up and go out naked to the balcony. Holding a glass of champagne, I look out at the sea, imagining I am a goddess in the moonlight. Perhaps someone else somewhere can see me too.

Hugh believes he is happy, I tell myself. My most selfless act would be to do nothing: leave him to his pleasure. Until it sours and rots. He'll come back, once his infatuation has run its course. We've been together too long for Hugh not to wind up crawling up the steps and slithering back into the house, if that is where I decide to wait for him. For now, I am still stuck on this stupid boat.

Glass and all, I toss the champagne into the sea.

DAY 10

I lie in the throuple's bed watching TV. Everything is supremely stupid. I laugh along at the murders and desperate searches. What a hilarious concept, exerting so much energy over a dead thing! Like launching a manhunt to find a candy bar wrapper. But when some very made-up women in bad lighting start smacking each other and pulling hair, something hits home and I turn the TV off.

The throuple, meanwhile, sleep most of the day. They're exhausted, they don't look well. They're not handling my bender with the pluck I'd hoped for. Now and then, I check to make sure they haven't peed on anything. Soon I'll have to rouse them to drink, eat. See, Hugh? See how much I care, how human I've become? One night without you and I'm already learning to bed drown, or whatever it's called.

But he doesn't want to be human, he wants to be something more. Not a god, no. He would never admit to that. Besides, he is already a god among artists. They revere him, study him.

The ship is supposed to dock somewhere today. I don't remember or care where right now, yet a cursory glance out the window reveals we are still at sea.

"Inclement weather," says a smooth voice over the loudspeaker. Unless the cruise director replaced their larynx, it's someone else talking now. Someone with more authority. "Poor visual conditions . . . Unfortunately at this time we are unable . . ." The ship isn't stopping, in other words.

I step out on the tiny Juliet balcony and look around. There's a skim of fog hovering over the water—for a moment, I think it's a miasma manifested by my grief. But we're sailing through it easily enough. In fact, I can see land through the mist, and bright, irregular stars.

Except it isn't mist. It smells like smoke and those aren't stars at all. The coast is burning. It's the war. And now we're adrift.

I rouse the throuple. "Go feed yourselves. Eat. But don't bring the food in here, I don't need to see that. Come back when you're done."

They nod sleepily. Their clothes mostly fit. All the bits are covered, anyway.

They leave and I'm alone. Well, in a way, I'm alone when they're with me. Without them, I'm a little more alone.

They come back scared. Someone in the buffet line was upset and saying upsetting things. About the war, I assume. But that's not it. People are missing, they say. The first three people they describe are actually themselves. But then they mention someone else too. I don't remember the name on the flier that stuck to my shoe, and they don't remember the flier at all. So who knows if it's the same one?

It finally dawns on me that something is wrong aboard this ship, something beyond my own personal hell. It turns out, it's actually hell for everyone. *We're on vacation!*

I release the throuple. I don't need them anymore. But I retain one of their wristbands so I can hold on to their room.

DAY 11

I put on my orgy trench coat and sunglasses and mesmerize, hypnotize—whatever word you want to use—an important-looking employee. All in white, more cake, only with a hat. Not the captain, they're too much work to access. But someone who knows things. They tell me there will be no more stops, we're all stuck aboard, which I already figured out. Also, there have indeed been a handful of disappearances.

"A handful? How many is a handful?" We're standing in the shade between some potted palms. There are pool sounds, sexy queer hip-hop is playing, made by one of those musicians accused of desecrating god with sexy naked men. I like it. The Christians are right, it makes me want to take my clothes off. But right now it's distracting.

"I don't know," the officer-or-whatever says. I don't know their title, I'm not a sailor. "It happens a lot in this business. Suicides, sometimes foul play. International waters . . . Whatever happens at sea . . ." Their eyes glaze over.

"That's Vegas."

Their eyes drift away from one another. "Right."

"Is someone murdering people?"

They blink. "No sign of foul play," they recite. "Seems like they fell overboard."

But there are guardrails. Suicide is possible but physically challenging.

Maybe Heaven's left a trail of mysteriously disappeared lovers. Maybe they plan to absorb Hugh's identity, then dispose of him. Hugh, I realize, *my* Hugh, might be in real danger. *Mortal* danger. If such a thing is possible. A new, deeply unpleasant sensation settles in. It's more acute than emptiness, with more static than sorrow. It's fear again, but of a sharper variety.

I suddenly wish I were better at computer things.

"Now look something up for me."

But I don't know Heaven's last name, and we soon find out that if you search "Heaven from LA," you mostly get a lot of pop songs and Instagram accounts for prophets and bakeries, none of which are attributed to the Heaven aboard this ship.

I send the officer-or-whatever back to work. Then I remove my trench coat and go stare at the water. Clouds swarm the sun. The ocean goes black. It's alive; I watch it move. The abyss is so absorbing. It's a welcome sort of terror. Then I take a nap in a candy-striped lounge chair by a heart-shaped pool.

By evening, I'm back to playing detective, and what

do detectives do? They spy. So it makes sense that I'm watching Hugh and Heaven go to dinner at a Sea Dragon restaurant. Apparently, you're allowed a lower-class plus-one, but not a plus-two. From a distance, I see black lacquered wood and giant ferns and prehistoric fronds, wooden masks and wicker. There's a canoe hanging from the ceiling. A boat on a boat.

I work my will over the host, who seats me at a table in the corner of my choice. My table is meant for six to eight people, but it's the perfect vantage point. I sit right in the middle with my sunglasses on. I am not cut out for invisibility, so if I must keep a low profile, I aim for "mysterious and aloof." But I'll never entirely "blend in." Not with the lights on, anyway.

And yet I am not only invisible but undetectable to the only one that matters: Hugh is here. He should sense my presence. He should smell me, for fuck's sake.

Over there, at their table, he looks happy in a bewildered sort of way. He doesn't say much. Meanwhile, Heaven drinks three glasses of something blood red and bubbling with a weird dried garnish, maybe a preserved starfish, or placenta. They talk and talk, gesturing with one hand, the other holding their cauldron-shaped cup. Hugh nods and nods and nods. In between monologues, Heaven scoops glistening bits of food into their mouth. Is that *bone marrow*? All that vegan sushi, just for show. I can't believe I ever fell for their lipstick schtick, with shiny hair and accessories. That's all it is, a bit of flimflam. There's nothing remarkable about Heaven, nothing at all, except for the one thing they can't tell anyone about. How that must eat them up.

Meanwhile, I order a drink that comes in its own little cauldron under a bell jar, and when the server lifts the lid, smoke billows out, real smoke. It's delightful. I order a second, just so I can watch it all again. The server looks confused, swapping one full cauldron for another. I just smile. The server smiles back primly, then disappears.

Now Heaven is taking selfies. They scoot closer to Hugh, and he actually *leans in*. He smiles, sort of. He's trying. The flash goes off.

A selfie. The two of them just took a selfie. The absurdity is too much, and for a moment, I simply can't grasp it. It's like trying to do complex equations in your head. The idea feels close, yet very far away.

This is not possible, what is happening right now.

Someone sits down at my table.

"Excuse me?" I say, but they're smiling like they know exactly where they are.

"Well, it's very nice to meet you as well." They appear not so much ageless as timeless, with angular, vulpine, yet racially ambiguous features, well suited to their triangular eyeglasses. All topped by a shock of white hair with a perfect fade on one side. They smell like a scent I once knew but have forgotten, like a mix of juniper and myrrh. They're one of us, an old one, I can tell.

"Have we met?"

"We have now." Their accent is British, how delightful. They hold out a long thin hand with elegant fingernails. "I'm Misha, I saw you alone and I thought, well there's a story."

Their eyes are brown with flecks of green and blue. Their smile is salacious: pointy, slightly crowded teeth. Look at those sexy teeth. I get the sense we might have similar hunting habits.

"Feeding well here?"

"Oh, I never want to leave." They smirk and I can't tell if it's a joke. Delight or doldrums.

None of us can leave right now, though I very much want to. But with Hugh beside me.

"Well, I just wanted to pop by. I'll leave you to it."

"Stay. At least have a drink."

"Well, if you insist. What's your flavor?"

"My what? Oh." I gesture at my body, my obvious beauty. I cross my legs. "You?"

They purse their lips. "My taste is a little harder to satisfy."

Now I'm curious. I look around the room, as if there are clues hidden in the restaurant somewhere. What are they looking for here?

Ah, I think I know. "I've got it."

"Do you? Tell me."

"Oh, you just want me to be wrong. But if I'm right, I'm surprised to find you here."

"Really?" Misha shrugs. Their suit is midnight blue,

a perfectly tailored illusion. I wonder what's underneath. "I suppose we all need a little change of scenery now and then. But I think you'd be surprised by what I've unearthed here."

I imagine Misha slinking around the ship like they've snuck into an enclosure housing certain rare birds. They clutch an untouched snifter of brandy for some reason, cooling in their hand, as they quietly observe the passengers who've gambled too high, cheated too long, sunk too low in their arguments.

Misha tells me they live in London, though they often travel to New York for work, which I envy.

"I'm thinking of moving abroad myself." Is this true? I hadn't thought about it until now. So I suppose it might be true.

"The Continent will suit you well." They look me over, and when their eyes pass my breasts, my nipples wake up.

What would I find in London? More fog, certainly, more delicious accents, plus museums and other old things, underground clubs. Stuffiness and peacoats. I do enjoy environments where open sluttiness is met with at least tacit approval, as in San Francisco, where there are nude bike rides and BDSM leather street fairs.

"What is your 'work?'"

"I'm a 'consultant,' as they say." Misha's fingers hook the air. Such sharp yet delicate nails. "I work for an agency that manages redundancies. It's quite horrible, really. A whole subterfuge to improve efficiency, when really we just come in and sack everyone." Misha shrugs and smirks, and once again, I can't tell if they're amused or sheepish.

"Is that a primal fear thing, or existential dread?"

"Hmm. A bit of both, really. Feeding the children versus the futility of it all, the utter meaninglessness of Sisyphean toil."

"Which do you like better?"

Misha thinks for a moment. "I really have to say, it depends so much on my mood, or what I consumed the day before. Primal is certainly more potent, but the existential has a long finish, it very much lingers on the palate."

I'm such a gobbler, I realize. I don't usually think about feeding with this level of nuance.

Suddenly Heaven rises and glides away from their table, Hugh drifting in their wake. There are whispers. Out of spite, I refuse to ogle Heaven's outfit.

Hugh looks bewildered. He's wrinkleless, as always. But I spot dark circles under his eyes.

Misha watches me watching him, pulls down their triangular glasses as if to get a better look. Except their eyewear is lensless, the frames are just an accessory. We all have perfect sight, after all.

"Hmm." They study Hugh. "That gentleman looks familiar." They toss their drink in a fake potted plant, then beckon the waiter to bring a fresh one.

"That's my husband."

The pair pass from the room without so much as a glance at me.

"And the other one?" Misha leans forward, squinting, playing with their glasses again.

"They met here."

"Ah. Bad luck, that."

"Have you ever met a shapeshifter before?"

Misha startles. "A what? Oh no. Shapeshifters are a lot of trouble, quite nasty. They're full of tricks. They're swindlers, really. Best avoided if possible, even by our kind." They gently claw my arm in solidarity.

Just as I feared. I feel hot and cold at once. Misha leans in, smiling, sampling.

"So sorry," they lean away, blushing. "Sometimes I just can't help myself, especially when the company is particularly delectable."

It's extremely bad form to prey on your own. Hugh would be appalled. But I shrug like I don't mind, even though I do, because Misha is so beautifully androgynous, their accent so crisp and refreshing. "But have you actually met one?"

"My dear, I've known all kinds. All kinds of trouble, that is." They chortle.

"Are they mortal, do you think?"

"Hmm. I *believe* they are."

* * *

Misha is confident they can locate Heaven on the internet.

"You just have to know *how* to look," they say. They're so much older than I am, but somehow they've mastered things like hashtags.

Suddenly our phones are full of photos and short videos taken from all over the ship, featuring every major attraction, even the ones I know Heaven never touched, with complementary outfits for each. I should expect this, but it still shocks me to see Hugh in some of the photos. He's blurry, only half in frame. There are also images of various skin products, shoes, champagne, vodka and other liquors, nail polish, etc. The merchandise is all tagged.

Hugh doesn't use social media, but his fans do, apparently. Some of them have even adopted his name and image as their own. They're talking about him in the comments, wondering what on earth he's doing aboard a cruise, is this some kind of consumer commentary? Where's his wife? one says, and I'm both gratified and offended. Yes, indeed, where am I? But also I'm not "a wife." I have my own identity . . . which now includes social media stalking my immortal beloved's new lover.

We scroll back to the pre-trip content. I don't know what I expect: To find the temple Heaven built in their own honor? Footage of all their lovers in cages? Or their graves? There are videos of Heaven making tea and talking, or doing their makeup, or brushing their hair while also talking talking talking. It's terribly boring. There's one where they're dancing in silk pajama shorts and fluffy slippers in what must be their bathroom, piles of mucky towels everywhere, too many toothbrushes jutting out of the hairy sink. Dogs yap and scream in the background. Heaven ignores them.

I pause over a clip where Heaven's face is blotchy and bloated. They dab their eyes with tissues while blathering on about toxic energy and sycophants, their gaze continuously drifting off camera. The clip has hundreds of thousands of views. There are several other crying clips, including one about something called IBS. How vile. I want Hugh to see it, but I know he never will.

All this time, I've kept my identity to myself. Heaven reveals every detail to the world, and the world, apparently, actually cares, and yet their identity is still a secret. No one on this app knows what they really are. Incredible.

Actually, what they really are is a creature better suited to these times than I am. That is one major difference between us.

Misha senses my disappointment and turns to me with a question on their face, different from the one they ask aloud. "Had enough?"

"More than enough."

Misha sighs. "This is why I live with pets instead of lovers. They last longer, which isn't very long at all."

"You have pets?"

They nod. "Oh yes, I have a bearded dragon and a hedgehog. Nothing too needy. I find it suits me well. They really are the best company, if you can get past the smell."

I've never considered a pet before. I find I'm considering all kinds of new things as I contemplate a rootless future, alone.

"Rebekah," Misha purrs, "would you like to join me for a hunt?"

"Thank you for the kind invitation, but . . ." I'm about to refuse when I realize, why shouldn't I? What's stopping me? "I happily accept."

"Well." Misha looks at me like I'm a bit odd, but they kind of like it. "That's wonderful. Shall we?"

I slide out of my seat. "So where are we going?"

Another vulpine grin. "You'll see." Misha offers me their arm.

* * *

Where do fear and desire merge? We travel down into the belly of the ship where there's a glass gymnasium, like a panopticon of physical torture, complete with a climbing wall that leads nowhere. Despite the hour, the place is packed. It stinks of desperation. Everywhere, bodies in stretchy fabrics are lunging, grinding, pedaling, clenching. They're all watching each other and pretending not to, cruising and competing at once. It's the most savage thing I've yet seen on this trip.

Misha sighs. "I miss the Roman gyms. No attire necessary."

I'm not such a fan of sweaty flesh as Misha. "What's here for me?" I murmur.

Misha's surprised. "My dear, look at you. You have what everyone here desires: beauty. Forever."

Just a glance reveals they're right: there are many eyes on me, sober eyes, portholes to little tunnels of longing. (Porthole is such an obscene word.) They want, they want, they want . . . And now they want me. I take it in—why not? We're in the middle of the melee, dressed like we're going to dinner but somehow wound up here by mistake. They can't help but notice us and our hotness. But their desire doesn't satisfy, it's bitter with envy.

Misha breathes deeply through their nose. "Mmm. Definitely existential. With a soupçon of self-loathing. One might say a bit heavy on the shame, but I don't shy away from a bolder palate."

I like listening to them talk. And I like watching them, I realize. The way their nose prickles. I tune in. They took a dirty little sip off me earlier, now it's my turn to be nasty. I smile, draw them closer.

"Oh my," Misha says as our gaze locks and I move in for a kiss, the whole gym watching us with a mix of curiosity and arousal, which levels out the envy for a moment. What a surprise to meet this gourmand, here of all places. And they're also an exhibitionist. I like that too.

There's too much sweat in here.

"Let's go somewhere else." I know just the place.

* * *

The movie theater is "free," but they still give you paper ticket stubs to hold. Nevertheless, so far it's the "realest" place on board: it smells like spoiled popcorn and sugar syrup. The floors are sticky. The employees are sparse and stuck in ugly maroon vests, even. They drag brooms, disappear just as a lone customer approaches the candy counter.

We're late, it's already started, which suits us just fine. The theater is deserted, there are only a few bodies in the seats, but we aren't here for them. Misha takes my hand as we fumble into our row at the back. On the screen is a campy horror flick where all the sluts get killed, the obviously gay person first, of course. It's a queer classic, despite the anti-slut message, simply because it enter-tains the idea that queers exist. There are a lot of cheesy one-liners, buckets of corn-syrup blood.

We look straight at the screen while our hands fish around in each other's laps. I try not to laugh, but then I think, *Why not?* and cackle so loudly, the humans get confused, think it's part of the film.

By the time the credits roll, we're twisted up in our seats, making out like lovers who know they're about to be wrenched apart.

I ask Misha if they want to go somewhere and fuck properly.

"I have an extensive skin-care regimen I need to get started on." They kiss my ear, then my neck.

This is a lie, of course. Misha knows I know that. Skin care? They want to leave me wanting. Plus, I suspect they're going to go sneak another feed before bed. Misha has quite the appetite, it seems.

But I don't have the patience for this right now, or maybe ever. If they expect me to push, they're disappointed. "Enjoy," I tell them, and catch them in one last kiss, my tongue signing all the things they've just refused. I leave them with their eyes half-open.

I realize I haven't thought about Heaven and Hugh for a few hours. Except now I am thinking about them. The relief and pleasure are gone. Even my clit is suddenly inactive, numb. I don't know where I'm going now, or what to do with myself.

Except, already, my body moves into stealth, skulking, sifting through smells and sounds. I'm tracking them. I have to know where they are, if Hugh is all right. If Hugh is still *Hugh*.

This is what my tracking gets me: I discover they're sharing Heaven's room now. That's their headquarters, so to speak. I stand outside the door and listen to the rumblings within. No sex sounds, only murmurs and snores. I know the rhythms of Hugh's sleep.

I'm not sure if I feel better or worse that they're just sleeping and not fucking.

Heaven wakes up. I hear them moving around, drinking from a plastic water bottle. Maybe they can smell me. Maybe not. In any case, they go back to bed.

DAY 12

Sliding past the pools in my crocheted bikini, I spot this gorgeous creature all in cream like the spume that made Aphrodite. I covet their sandals. They turn my way, smirking. Wait, I know that smirk. Now comes a wink, in my direction. This is no angel lady killer, no demon lover. It's Heaven, of course, playing their little games. I scowl and swallow spit. This is a warning perhaps—they know I've been watching.

I look for Hugh. Where have they stashed him?

Heaven struts past and someone drops their mimosa into the pool. They settle in at the thatched-roof bar where the bartenders are pouring rum and tequila into hollowed-out pineapples. They order something with a big fruit-skewer garnish. Their hair shifts ever so softly, camouflaging, copying my own, but with more curl. We kind of look like siblings now. Somehow this is both hot and insulting, like they're demonstrating how my hair *should* be.

Heaven winks at me again. So much winking! Their

face is theirs again, luscious beard and all. I admit it, they're winning.

I slink over to the bar and take a seat beside them. They smell like expensive unscented sunblock and freesia.

"I didn't think you'd give him up," Heaven says.

For once, we're speaking frankly, then. The California uptalk is gone too. Is this the "real" Heaven? Does such a person even exist?

"He doesn't belong to me."

Heaven smiles like they're embarrassed for me.

"What are you up to?"

"Up to? Me?" Today their nails are a soft yellow. Heaven tosses their hair, and it falls like silk over their shoulder, the curls letting go, flowing loose. How do they get it to shine like that? "What would your name be if you were a pirate?"

I have honestly never considered this question. "Couldn't I keep my name?"

"If you want. I thought you had more imagination than that."

"Sorry to disappoint."

"Are you going to keep spying on us?"

"What do you want, Heaven?"

They look confused. "You mean, like, in life?" The uptalk is creeping back in. "Well, I'm really trying to achieve symbiosis."

I'm not sure if this is a taunt or a joke, or if they're actually serious. How could they be serious? Who talks this way?

I'm the shark. I am ancient. I am the predator. I will not be bested on a floating carnival by some social-climbing, shapeshifting pedestrian.

"Will you be there?"

"Where?"

Heaven points. That's when I see it: one of those kiosk screen things announcing a special guest speaker tonight. It's Hugh. There's *Lilitu*, taken in 1975, his most famous piece, and there's Hugh's in-profile headshot, where he's eternally brooding like Hades. This cannot be real. It's a prank. The kiosk has been hacked. Hugh doesn't do public speaking, especially not impromptu, especially not when it's absolutely unnecessary, with no possible benefit to his desires.

"They had to bump someone else, some performer," Heaven whispers, all conspiratorial. "And Hugo didn't want to at first. He's so humble and shy! He doesn't want a fuss." They preen with pride. "So, you'll be there in support, right?"

Well, Heaven has done it. They've found a way to get me to sit through an art lecture.

* * *

I arrive early and already the auditorium is abuzz. Only the seats at the back are free. I wonder if Misha is here somewhere, if they can sniff me out, my perfume of fear and failure. My shoulders sink, I scoot lower in my seat.

When I met Hugh . . . I reach my hand through time, dip into the nebula of the Before, sift through the sand,

and come up with . . . nothing. I can't quite remember when I met him exactly, which is probably why I haven't told the story already. There is no Before Hugh anymore.

Oh for fuck's sake, I'm waxing poetic here.

There's an introduction, of course, performed by some nondescript person of no importance. Then, the audience shrieks and applauds. It's Hugh up there, and yet it isn't. He's dressed all in black, the suit impeccably tailored as always, though I don't recognize it from his wardrobe. His skin looks weird—too smooth, too uniform and shiny, like it's not real. I imagine Heaven coating his face with liquid plastic, then applying paint, blending with brushes, building him a mask.

Or maybe it really is a mask. What if it's not him at all? What if it's Heaven up there? What if they've taken him?

But then he begins, sputtering, with lots of "uhs" and "umms," and there's no doubt. Relief! It is Hugh after all. He mumbles through the story he's told a thousand times, quite literally. Everyone is still and quiet, no one so much as coughs. Then he shows slides. Slides! Piece after piece, no dates or titles of course. Meanwhile, Hugh monotones along. What he says, if you can make it out, doesn't align with what's on the screen. He's telling one story, the images recount another. But it doesn't matter, they'll revel in this dissonance, finding great intentionality behind it. It's deliberately arduous, like a religious experience. This is what they're all here for.

Finally, he arrives at the slide they're waiting for, the one famous piece everyone can feel proud of recognizing. There's a collective intake of breath: there it is, wall-sized, with the artist right beside it. So what if it isn't the real thing? Little fireworks pop off silently—the audience is tapping away, taking bad photos. But photos of something famous are still good even when they're bad.

In *Lilitu*, a man looks out a window. He's standing within what appear to be black curtains, but there are no curtains, it's a cape of darkness. The window is dusty, cracked. The state of the wall and window ledge suggests a war-torn building. The man is looking right into the light, and in return, the light reveals his face, and it is broken. It's his face, really, that makes the photo. The story of this man is one of loss. The scent of his grief draws Hugh to him. He's feeding as he's taking the photo. As the shutter clicks, he grows fat off this man's pain at losing his child, his family. And then an artsy little slice of the world loses its mind over this image because it's so terribly sad and wrong and liking it feels like doing something about all the terribly sad and wrong things no one can do anything about.

Hugh isn't in the photo of course, but we know he's there, behind the camera. *Lilitu* is a Babylonian soul sucker or something. How many theses have been written about that damn title and what it's trying to say about death, war, poverty, all that? Everyone looking at it thinks, "This is what the artist sees; this is how he sees the world. We're looking through his eyes, the eyes of a great artist." So, too, the audience drinks up the subject's pain. What idiots. Really, it's the closest he's ever come to a self-portrait. The artist who made this is not the same one Heaven promised Hugh he could be.

The photograph is too big and too bright. It's not supposed to be lit like this. They haven't even dimmed the lights in the auditorium. What amateurs. Hugh looks up at it, his gaze climbing the screen. He faces his subject, who's big enough to swallow him. Fitting. The lost father is looking through the window, and Hugh is on the other side, looking back. His posture, his expression—they intimate great pain. He's become a mirror of the father.

Hugh stares up at the slide and he doesn't say anything. The silence stretches on, the tension swells to fill the room. Finally, he turns with an anguished look toward the audience. He's reliving the moment he took the photo, they all think. He's grappling with his own humanity, and they're not wrong about that part.

First, a sniffle. Then another. Someone lets loose a wail. Then a tsunami of screams and applause.

Hugh has found me. I stare right back, the only one here who truly *sees*, as the humans fizz with pure, pathetic sadness. Several people are weeping.

Up on stage, haloed by misery, Hugh shines. He can't help it, my love; he's feeding, tenderly yet steadily. It's just too much to resist. I'm the only one who bears witness to this ecstasy. It's divine and obscene all at once—how he gorges. His head lolls forward and back. These humans have willingly crammed themselves in like cattle, just to see him. They have come to be milked. There's more crying.

Hugh's eyes find me again. He's growing soft now, overfed. I'm the one who understands. This is between us.

I am a bird that flew into a window. I desire him— how could I not? Also, my ears are ringing, and I feel weak. This isn't you, my love. This isn't my love. Why do you need to be anyone else?

A terrible thought rises like a bloody moon: I'm feeding him too. I'm feeding him my anguish right now, and neither of us can make it stop. I wonder if mine is different, if he can taste it, if it has a different flavor when it's someone you love.

He looks at me, and he knows I know. His face falls. No more softness, no more joy. He looks haggard.

More phones flash. This is all surely being filmed. Soon, there will be articles posted to the internet about this moment of collective feeling and communal grief, where the artist is rendered mute by the insufferable power of his own work. It's a kind of communion with the audience, they'll say. On a cruise ship no less! *We're on vacation!* They'll decide it's really about this or that current tragedy or slow-boiling holocaust.

Suddenly, Hugh steps backward and disappears. The audience gasps. The stage is empty, but he's still there, cloaked under the black wing of stage right. Only *Lilitu* remains. The photo gets the final word, a conclusion in and of itself.

A pause, then rolling thunder of applause and cries, shrieks, many more wails, whistles, ululating, finger snaps. They love it. *Hurt us again*, the audience begs. *Drain us dry.*

The person who introduced Hugh at the start of this thing comes back out, beaming yet sheepish, fully aware the fervor has nothing to do with them. They stoop and bow toward the wing through which Hugh has at last exited the stage, then say something into the mic, but the audience is water, they wash the host away.

And now I want very much to get the fuck out of here. I want to eat and get eaten out, maybe by Misha. Or maybe throw things, or sink to the bottom of a pool and linger there.

People are milling about the stage, waiting for a private audience with Hugh. The crowd parts for Heaven, who struts up in a showstopper dress with a slit up to the hip, hair rippling. Their makeup is ancient Egyptian, their heels are thin blades of hard plastic that look like crystal. Everyone gawks.

Heaven takes the stage. They pageant-smile, posing for the paparazzi in their mind: the artist's lover, tall as a titan, waving like a dictator's wife. More phones flash. I hope Heaven is prepared to keep track of Hugh's phone and handwash his silk socks. Of course, I know Heaven will do no such things. What a selfish beast. I almost admire them.

"Thank you!" Heaven cries. Their voice soars over the crowd.

Hugh reemerges, from stage left this time. He grasps Heaven's arm like a buoy. The audience stomps and whistles and claps their hands sore. Heaven beams. Hugh is stuffed. He's sleepy and morose. But Heaven licks their plate clean.

As the crowd clots closer to the stage, I rise and slip out. I wish I could turn into an actual albatross. Or a bat. I wish I could fly away.

* * *

The sea is getting bigger somehow, like the land is just our imagination. I have this terrible feeling we're lost. The passengers, too, sense something is wrong. I hear them in the passageways, sniping and snarking at each other. The sun comes out, bold as brass, and still we don't stop. We're stuck here, the three of us, with no choice but to feed from the same flock.

Except I don't eat. I've lost my taste for it again. I don't rest either. All I do is lurk and linger. It's terrifically boring, and I use up what's left of my reserves to enchant those who get spooked when they stumble upon me lurking and lingering. Peering around the corner and down the sliver of a passageway I'm not supposed to access, at the end of which is Heaven and Hugh's door. Doorway to Heaven. Oh, will the puns ever end?

Other people come out of H+H's room. (Is that their celebrity couple name?) People I never see going in. They wear brand-new clothes and stink of fermented apples. They're all Heaven, of course, zipped in there. We're shells and they're a hermit crab. How and why does Heaven choose? I wonder. Are these figures recognizable to the pop culture-consuming hordes aboard this ship? Do they have VIP passes, literally and figuratively?

Or maybe Heaven chooses at random, just for shits and giggles. But I very much doubt that. Heaven has taste. And ambition, one of the worst of their very-human qualities. A stomach for attention that's never full is a very-human quality too.

I wait and I wait. I pretend I'm a snake or a cat, a creature of infinite patience. But Hugh doesn't come out. I imagine he's tied up, dangling off the balcony like a tuna. I slink around the corner, tiptoe closer. If Hugh were to look through the peephole right now, he'd spot me. How embarrassing, to get caught out caring so fucking much, debasing myself. I stalk because I care! But it's a risk I'm willing to take, I suppose. I'm not sure why, or what I expect to happen. Hugh will emerge eventually, and then? I don't know, I don't know. My thoughts are swampy. I mean, murky. It's the hunger talking.

I'm too close; I can smell him in there, the musky tobacco of his ennui. Heaven may have turned him into some kind of mystic of self-deception and optimistic denial, but they can't change who he is at his core. That is what his scent tells me, sure as a hound can smell cancer and menses. He's still in there.

A rustling. The door handle quivers. I press myself flat, lizard-like, against the wall. When the door opens, it shields me, though the knob rams into my gut. Doesn't he smell me? Sense me? Hugh moves down the passageway without hesitation. If he knows I'm here, he's not letting on. But he's slow. His color is off, his clothes look too big. Despite the smorgasbord, he's diminished. It's all too much for him, his constitution is too frail.

I never asked him to perform publicly. I provided closets to conceal him, beds to slip beneath. How selfish, Heaven's hunger. They don't love Hugh; they will never look out for him. And isn't that what love is, in the human sense? Looking out for someone's best interest, even when it conflicts with your own?

I creep along behind him. Those coming toward us see me and freeze, but Hugh doesn't even notice them. He brings me to the room we shared at the start of this trip. Hugh stands there like he's trying to remember how to open the door. Eventually, he sighs and slips away, and I shadow his shadow.

Back in Heaven's room, he rummages around for a few minutes. It sounds like a rat's nest in there. Then he comes out with a book under his arm. He's wearing the sunglasses I gave him.

I tail him to the elevator. Obviously, I don't get in with him, I just wait to see which floor he lands on. Down the numbers go. I descend after him and find myself in a cavernous lower deck. There are no windows. Wisps of smoke pass, like shadow prisms. It's a smoking lounge, a den of iniquity. No poppy though, sadly. I believe I smoked opium once or twice, even though drugs have no effect on me. But the idea is familiar; my tongue tastes the memory of the smoke. I enjoy the art of it, like a tea ceremony.

Hugh was made to sit and smoke in a suit. Or wear a smoking jacket. He looks like a magazine ad. He looks like the loneliest, most dapper man in the world. Where's Heaven? The fact that they're apart this close to the end of the trip suggests a rift. Or they intend to leave together, so they're relaxed, they have endless time to spend in each other's company. They assume the end will come, we will arrive somewhere. And then . . . I imagine Hugh and Heaven holding hands on the plane, both in sunglasses. I see them collecting their baggage, sliding into a rideshare. Hugh will send for the rest of his wardrobe.

It's ridiculous, impossible, this ending. This is not my life. I refuse this story.

DAY 13

In the evening, I force myself to hunt even though my heart—or is it my clit?—still isn't in it. Even my libido has shrunk to a button. And this damn manacle is chafing again. I'm distracted, graceless. Wandering one of the malls, looking for things to pocket, I run into someone. Literally—I crash into them, or they into me. I snarl.

"Rebekah? Rebekah, oh my god, hi!"

How do they know my name? I'm suspicious. I sniff. Is this Heaven?

A tug on my arm sucks me into a cephalopodic group hug. I'm swallowed by this posse of thirty-somethings with impeccable teeth and delicate rings of gold cinched to their noses. None of them look at all familiar, and you'd think I'd remember them, they're so beautiful.

"From the . . . party. Remember?" They beam.

They tell me all their names, which are just sounds, and I nod. They offer their adoration freely, I don't even have to try. It's as if they're holding a handblown glass straw to my lips, urging me to drink until I feel—if not better, at least something different.

"We're going to see this performance artist. Is that where you're headed?"

I have never voluntarily witnessed performance art. Isn't all art a performance of some sort anyway? Never mind, that's the kind of thing Hugh would say.

But Hugh might be there. If he is, though, then so is his new paramour. Maybe I don't want to see either half of H+H right now. I'm having feelings and it hurts and I want it to stop.

But I don't want to be rid of this group just yet. I can always steer them away from the show, I reason. So I tell the orgy leftovers to lead the way, and off we go to a child's rainbow ball pit with adults milling about the edge, shifting and staring like they're contemplating jumping in. No one is talking. There's no sign of Heaven or Hugh. And then I peer inside the pit: a skeletal figure with a shaved head is sitting on something under the balls, which appear gray and black in the dark. They don't seem to know we're there. Fish-eyed, three fingers in their mouth, they slowly remove one wet screw after another. After another. They discard the screws casually, dropping them in the pit.

I hate performance art. I turn to the leftovers—they're engrossed of course.

"What incredible commentary," says one.

"Absolutely," says another.

"Capitalism," nods the third.

"What would Hugo think?" This is directed at me.

"What?"

"Do you think he'll be here?" they whisper.

So that's why they remember me. My sexual acrobatics have nothing to do with it, it's all about getting closer to Hugh. Is everyone on this ship obsessed with him?

"What?" I say a little too loudly, and there are glares. I'm disrupting the atmosphere.

"Is he here?" They swivel and search.

This attention tastes like shit. Fuck me, I'm on a barge of starfuckers and I'm not the star. I'm in hell. And Hugh isn't even here with me. He's living a completely different life right now, aboard the same garbage barge.

"Fuck it," I say, and someone dares to "shh" me, but I can't tell who.

There are still more wet screws coming out of the human in the ball pit. That's it, I'm leaving.

* * *

The orgy leftovers' blatant machinations are a wake-up call. I have a look at myself: I don't recognize this self who follows people around. Rebekah is powerful, irresistible. She can't let Heaven diminish her like this.

I head to the upper deck to stand in the wind, the way we did on our first night, sucked in by the noise of the sea machine. I close my eyes against the air. I am a force of nature, too, I think.

I sense someone is there. There's a familiar scent—it must be Hugh. I wait for him to close in.

But he doesn't come, and finally I turn to see two figures, wrestling, and one of them lifts the other headfirst over the guardrail. There's no sound or flash. There's no great wave. Weightless, they simply disappear.

The figure still standing there turns to me. I can't make out their face. A pause, then they're running my way. I don't have time to react, I just open my mouth and nothing comes out.

The wind pours over me. But there's no one there. No one is coming.

* * *

After that, I put on a dress that's like a second skin and go rake my claws through the muck of the casino located in the bowels of the ship. There are cocktail waiters and no windows, just like the real thing, only this one smells like chlorine instead of cigarettes. Cards hiss, levers crank, coins rattle like chains. I don't pick, I let them draw me like that weeping woman drew Hugh in the alleyway in Istanbul. I wish we'd stayed there. I want to hunt in ancient cities.

Meanwhile, I prowl about the gambling floor, catching eyes, taking filthy little sips off everyone, hitting off them again and again, when I spot Misha. They beckon but I don't move, making it clear who needs to come to whom now. Also, I want to watch them walk.

They're swimming in black and red folds, like a paper lantern, with open-toed platforms. They look, in a word, fabulous.

"Enjoying the scenery?"

"I just got here," I lie.

"Join me for a game?"

"I don't gamble." I smile. We both know why I'm here.

Misha smiles too. It's a predator's smile.

"That shapeshifter, have they still got your husband in their clutches?" I realize they're overfed, drunk. They're on a binge. "Uncouth," Hugh would say. "What revolting manners." But Misha doesn't seem at all self-conscious about it this time, or even apologetic.

Instead, they try to needle more emotions out of me. "But you're alone, aren't you?" Their accent is suddenly Slavic.

Misha's milking me right now. Their refinement is a mask. I could just reach over right now and casually remove their jaw. But I wouldn't want to get blood on my outfit.

"Where are you from?"

"Oh, here and there," they say. "Who knows, after so long?"

"So long where? How did you become . . . what you are?"

"What we are," Misha corrects, at once obsequious yet condescending, like a concierge.

"What *we* are, fine. How did it happen?" I still want to get something out of this, but Misha doesn't want to give.

Their eyes follow something behind me. Slim, wet mouth ajar. They don't blink. "Please excuse me," Misha murmurs and scuttles off, closing in like a spider. The prey doesn't see it coming. Misha feeds until they fall down.

* * *

I leave the casino in search of another hunting ground. I am alone, blessedly alone, and on the prowl. I want to forget Misha and pig out.

It dawns on me the distaste they inspire—that's how Hugh feels about me. I'm grotesque.

Of course, that's only his point of view, influenced by personal proclivities and weaknesses. Again, I am objectively hot. I have, if not taste, then at least some pizazz. Getting eaten by me would be the best thing that ever happened to you.

I hypnotize and seduce my way into a black-tie dinner where my kind—those with Albatross manacles—are not allowed. Scent of death in the overly air-conditioned air: steak and lobster, caviar, raw fish, and cooked snails soaked in coagulating butter. Seafood is so grotesque.

The guests are older—seasoned. Silvery white. The ones with the most money, inherited wealth mostly. I can smell it, the children purchased overseas, some reaped and sown from surrogates in India, all currently at home with their Haitian and Filipina nannies. They aren't nervous like the plebs down below. Money is unsinkable.

Oh, and there's a piano, oh god, there's a piano!

Which someone in drag is playing on, with zero finesse.

I'm underdressed but I hold myself like I'm not, like I belong there. I'm the guest of honor, in fact. Soon a man with a microphone is announcing just that, and everyone applauds wildly—*they weren't expecting a special guest! What a treat! Is it someone famous?*—as I cast my spell over the room. And then I do a full striptease, which ends with a Russian split on the piano, and the crowd goes absolutely berserk. They start stripping of their own accord—they're freaks, these high-class crowds. Not because they're queer, because they can only do this here, at sea, away from neighbors, nannies, mothers-in-law, and random strangers with videophones. Really, I'm doing them a favor, drawing out their desire like a venom. They are guiltless, utterly free. Tomorrow they will be exhausted and confused, yet euphoric. My touch, my kiss, is a gift.

I leave them mostly naked and face down, asleep, the pianist, too, and the waitstaff. Some of the kitchen crew did escape and are enjoying a well-earned break.

Am I sated? Have I had enough? I don't know. I'm wobbly.

Suddenly the piano thunders and nearly knocks me down. A figure is leaning over the keys like the ivory's made of flesh, fingers digging in. I have to admit, they're pretty good. Dark hair covers the face. What song is this? Hugh would know. The hair looks like mine. I sniff: petrichor this time. That's my scent.

They're here. They've been here all along.

Heaven tosses their hair like they're on stage. Their face is my face. That's my smug look. That's my body they're zipped into. I've been robbed.

"Trickster!" I scream, and the music stops. I'm drunk on the whole party. I'm over-overfull.

Heaven stands up and I take in my own self—quite mesmerizing—my lovely countenance, mouth stretched into someone else's smirk. I know it's Heaven. I know it's a mirage, but I seem so intoxicatingly real. For the love of god, they even smell like me, and they're wearing an absolutely killer outfit: navy-blue dupion silk pants, high on the waist, wide leg, with peep-toe satin heels, a chartreuse charmeuse bustier-style top, a stylized jaguar appliqué lunging from the rib. All this paired with a magenta lip, dark-blue triangles of liquid eyeliner I really have to try. As I said, who hasn't imagined fucking themself? I'm not talking twin porn, I mean you and your clone. Think about it. Right? Also, if I get them naked, I can take those clothes.

"Hiiiiii," they/she/I say. Oh, they are enjoying themself. "Did you have a nice dinner?" Heaven wants me to know they saw everything, they know all about my gluttony. They're a bully, I think, another shame eater.

I smirk. I am tremendous. "Yes, I did."

Heaven never misses a beat. "You up for some dessert?" They strike a pose, hand on hip, contrapposto. Damn, I look good.

* * *

If you're into the sex clone idea, imagine this (and if you're not, you can skip this part, I suppose): Heaven matches my every move, anticipating me the way only someone who's truly inside you can, to the point that I almost believe I am truly fucking myself, and for a few minutes, it is absolutely perverse and glorious and surreal. Like a fever dream. I get to watch myself come.

Then it's over and Heaven is Heaven again and I remember that I hate them. It felt like a dream because it was—it's an illusion. That's why Heaven is smiling, so smug, like they know exactly what I'm thinking. Their long, elegant feet dangle over the end of the bed.

I notice the room is destroyed. We even shredded the curtains. Heaven observes the same. We lock eyes and laugh. We laugh until our cheeks ache. Then, we go quiet. Gaze still latched. We're both naked, supine—a vulnerable position. I chide myself. A hunter should know better than to expose her soft underbelly.

"Why me?" I say, and roll onto my stomach. From here, I could push off the bed and land on the ceiling.

"You?" They're so coy. Maybe the ambition is a lie, they have no end goal. They just enjoy playing games.

"Why my body?"

"Do you remember when you asked if I could turn into monsters?" They sound pouty and offended; I've brought back a bad memory. "I started wondering, actually, what would happen if I turned into *you*? And

I thought you might not like what I would do, as you. Then I tried it. Oh my god! It's like, so delicious, but you're never full. You're not necessarily hungry, not all the time, but it's always *so* good, the way things taste when you're starving. You know?"

These words have teeth. They chose me because, to them, *I* am the monster. And when they adopt my form, my power comes with it. I'm genuinely shocked by this; this is much more than a costume change. I didn't know shapeshifters could do that—I barely knew they existed. Then again, if Heaven becomes a fish, they surely swim. As a bird, they must fly. And lay eggs too, probably.

Now I begin to wonder if I have in fact been the target this whole time: Heaven deliberately isolates Hugh from me, transforms him into bait to lure me, track me, control me. They know they have nothing else to offer, that Hugh is all I want or care for. Heaven's using him to draw me in, so they can make *me* their pet. Or steal my life. Or both. Ah hah, I knew I was the protagonist!

"Heaven, what happens to the people you mimic?"

Heaven feigns confusion. "I dunno. Nothing happens to them."

"But if you wanted to take over someone's life permanently, then what?"

Heaven is silent. They don't have to say it: I already know they disappear. Perhaps Heaven has even "disappeared" some of the bodies aboard this ship. Who was that, dumping one overboard?

We have no secrets now. Which means *danger*. *I* might be going overboard. A flash of peasants with torches and pitch, dead hens and a coffin full of splinters. Heaven plans to destroy me.

They're moving in. I summon my strength like Thor calls his hammer. (Oh my god, how do I know this nerdy shit?) This may be the fight of my life.

"You've actually taught me a lot," they say.

"I'm not a teacher," I scoff.

"Really, though." They want to tell me all the terrible things they learned from me in order to taunt me, or guilt-trip me or something. But I don't care. I can't help it if I'm an inspiration, one way or another. I am a delectable beast—the taste depends on you.

And suddenly they're me again. It's like watching a flower bloom at an unnatural speed. I trace my nail down the length of their arm—my arm. God, I have great skin.

We smile with the same mouth.

At first, we wrestle in our human forms, naked as Greeks. And then, they change. I am Leto, they are the swan, swaddling the body of a god. They turn into an emerald-green cobra, which I don't think exists in the wild, and sink their fangs into my arm, pumping me full of venom. My arm swells and goes purple. I grab them by the tail and swing. When I let go, there's nothing. They're gone. *Bzzzt*! A black fly goes right for my eyeball. I swipe at it, the fly hits the wall, and now an owl tears around the room, shedding feathers, screaming and knocking things over. They dive-bomb and claw my scalp and the blood flows down my face. I reach out, totally blinded by the blood, mind you, and—*lucky me!*—I grasp the owl by the talons, which shred my flesh, and swing the body down like a chicken, seamlessly transitioning hand-to-hand. I grip the neck, I have both hands on the owl's neck. It's scaly and slippery, and suddenly there's a salmon slipping out of my grasp. They're headed for the sea! Even though the door to the balcony is closed, and it's a long way down. I don't have time to rationalize. Desperately, I lunge, casting my body over the slick fish body, and it wriggles under me, then shrinks. Something prickles like tiny cacti. I sit up and there's a spider, hairy and big as my hand. The spider makes a run for it, heads up the wall. Ah hah, a fatal mistake. I crawl after them and pluck it from the corner and squeeze. It bites me, I drop it.

I follow the spider to the floor and find myself instead facing a massive, slavering black dog with an ugly lip. Its growl rumbles. The fur looks soft and sleek, just like Heaven's hair. Lunge. Teeth in my neck, a terrible smell of blood and dog saliva. I punch the stomach, grasp the ribs, and push until there's a *crack* and a whimper. The body shrinks. I grab the neck and hold on. The neck turns to a snake in my fists, but I don't let go. It wriggles and shakes, ripples, turns to slime, but I hold fast to the stinging jelly, and when I feel it harden, turning to bone, or vertebrae, I snap it in two. Then I break it into pieces. The whole thing, I break it up. It's a bloody, slimy mess of different parts. A slime salad. I don't even realize I'm screaming. Or that there are viscera and fish scales on the ceiling. And all over me. I'm still naked, and my arm looks like an eggplant, the other one is shredded. I'm missing a few fingers and patches of scalp, but I'm already healing.

I hover and wait for the lumps to turn back into a person, but it doesn't change. And suddenly I don't feel so good about this, like all I did was kill a vulnerable thing, a jellyfish or a bird or something, even though I know that chum over there is no bird. These are the remains of a powerful and dangerous being who wears my skin and does things I do not do.

I scoop it all up as best I can and pour it off the balcony into the abyss. From primordial sea to primordial sea. I imagine the ocean somehow fertilizing the bits, a crab growing out of the neck, with giant spindly legs. It's a mistake; I should've burned the remains. There must be a furnace somewhere. But it's too late now.

I shower, dress fast, all in black, and flee.

* * *

It would be courteous of me to go find Hugh and tell him I murdered his lover. On some level, he'll understand. Hugh is old world. He may be passive, squeamish about the gooey parts, but he knows I have a right to vanquish a rival of this degree, let alone a threat to my survival.

But I'm not going to do that.

I seduce another officer. The hard part is finding one, believe me. The staff have had it. They're all hiding out, praying tomorrow they'll be rid of their fellows, who piss in the pools. Observing humans, any humans, up close for too long always leads to disgust, even among their own kind.

Nevertheless, I wonder what it's like when it's just the crew aboard, if they play music and have parties. Orgies, even. I imagine staying on as a stowaway. I could charm my way into an actual position, pose as the captain if I wanted to. Turn pirate—no one would ever suspect a pirate cruise ship.

But this ship is just a big gassy coffin. The endless confinement makes me want to scream.

So I twist and turn my way through the inner lab-yrinthian passageways like I'm finally going to find the ship's brain. I employ some charm along the way, to avoid questions. But when I see her, the rest requires no particular power. She's cute, with her butch haircut, the stark white of her uniform, and she stares hungrily at me of her own accord, which I like best. I bite my lip. All the crew are half-starved, half-mad by this point.

Her cabin is shared, with bunk beds squeezed between the walls. Wet towels hang off the ladder. Alto-gether, it looks like the closet some orphans hide out in. But I feel secure in this small space, with this new lover, who is toned and strong and eager to toss me around, show off her moves. This is exactly what I need. We fuck like the world is ending. And maybe it is; every moment, the world *is* ending for someone.

Eventually, she sleeps. I linger, though the bed is too small. I imagine little fruiting bits of Heaven waiting for me down below, in a bed of sand. Well, what can I do but get back on land as soon as possible?

I think maybe I've gotten wiser on this trip, if such a thing is possible. I feel . . . enriched, as if with minerals. Perhaps it was the vanquishing. Maybe I should do a bit more vanquishing now and then, where it's deserved.

Where is Hugh now? Waiting for Heaven, I suspect. He won't want to leave alone. I imagine him seated on a soft pink couch shaped like a conch, slim legs crossed, jacket open. He broods like a saint, a whiff of blood and anorexia. He'll be waiting a long time. Yes, I pity him. But pity and desire are not neighbors.

I leave the officer, the first mate, last mate—whoever she is, she's sleeping soundly. I wander the ship. It's supposed to be the last night, after all. I am not looking for Hugh, but I'm also not *not* looking for him. It's very late, the only ones out are sad drunks in silk kimonos, contemplating another drink or tossing themselves overboard. Which, again, requires athletic feats beyond their capabilities. Not everyone wants to go home. *We're on vacation!*

Sputtering fireworks go off like spectacular farts, crackling then falling away into the sea, as if to underline their own pointlessness. A sad person in a clamshell bikini top offers me their wristband with barely a glance. I exert no influence, expend no energy on a seduction, they're just that drunk. And depressed. I can't help it, I think of Hugh again. Maybe he's passing some other desperate drinkers somewhere right now, picking and choosing, sampling a little of each. Or maybe he's looking for Heaven. Well, he'll never find them.

I wonder if, in a hundred years, I'll forget him. No, that seems impossible. Maybe two hundred. That might be long enough to forget. It's hard to say, I'm not good with time.

The sad drunkard's cabin is on a lower level, down a horror-movie passageway lined with tiny doors, no windows, like solitary confinement for children. It's as bad as the skipper-or-whoever's quarters, but it'll have to do. The room is untidy but mostly empty. It smells faintly of vomit. Maybe there's a candle somewhere.

I lie on the soiled bed. All I have is what's on me: these clothes, shoes, a grubby wristband, that's it. I'm not even sure where my phone is now, to be honest. I don't have my passport with the fake birthday and our address in San Francisco.

I've made a decision: if and when the ship docks, I'm not going to the airport with all the vacationers. I'm going to roam the lands of Eastern Europe on a Vespa. I will open the doors wide to my memories, call them in. Also, I want to see some vertiginous castles. I want to creep over the stone walls in the night, bare-breasted,

bait for some weak man who cannot resist devilish temp-
tation. I'll make a meal of him, leave him naked and
unconscious. If he has any cash on him, I'll take that too.
And his car keys. What pleasure, to consider how human
things are useful but not necessary. How easily they can
be discarded or traded.

The irony is, I'm not human enough for Hugh, even
though I domesticated myself for him. Fixed in one spot,
with one companion, with a *job* of all things, when I
could have made my way around the world many times
over by now. How many incredible meals and fucks have
I missed out on?

A storm descends like the wrath of old gods. Maybe
the sea is angry I killed Heaven, or it doesn't like the taste
of them. The lightning flashes like there are paparazzi
outside the porthole. The ship tilts, tips so slowly, it's
almost imperceptible, the world is just veering slightly to
one side, that's all, a heavy head on a tired neck.

Suddenly I'm standing sideways. The motel art on
the wall is crooked. The room lurches to the left; the
world is untethered. I hear screams. And then I'm on the
floor. There's glass breaking and what sounds like a bag
of apples rolling around. This is it, we've hit an iceberg
at last. Except there are no icebergs out here. What there
is "out here" is war. It's the war, we've been hit. Now
we're tipping the other way as the ship rights itself. More
screams. The storm is storming. The ship is a whale's
cradle.

There's a knock at the door. How did he find me? But it's just staff, knees bent, feet wide, a youth with freckles and muscles, checking to make sure I'm all right. There's a little confusion, I'm not Mr. So-and-so? No, I'm not. I smile. Eyes lock. Click, like handcuffs. Please, won't you come in? Just like that. It's that easy.

After this fuck and feed, I'm done for the night, I swear. I'm full.

The soothing voice keeps telling me to stay in my quarters. Well, not just me, everyone. The same voice who lied about the weather reassures us that everything is fine and perfectly safe, and the medical team is treating all the people who've been injured by the lurch, which was just the safety gears kicking in to keep us in place. Perfectly normal, all apologies. No explosions. Repeat, there's *no* explosion. We're still scheduled to dock tomorrow. *In the meantime, the stewards are delivering a round of champagne!*

I don't know what to believe, so I venture out to watch the storm. It feels like we're not moving, the sea's shoving us on all sides. The sky strikes, furious with lightning. I taste brine and it's strange, to taste so much with my tongue.

This is the first time I've been truly alone on this trip; it's just me now.

Somewhere there's land I can't see. Maybe there are mountains—I would enjoy a mountain. One way or another, I'll get there. There are lifeboats hanging off the sides of this thing; I could find a cute crew member to pilot it for me. For me, nothing is impossible.

And then there he is, squinting, the wind parting his hair in unflattering ways. Maybe it's thinned, maybe he hasn't fed enough. Ah, but that's none of my concern. Hugh has to fend for himself.

He's fighting to reach me, jacket wings open, the buttons parting down his shirt. I could help. The wind is making less of an impression on me. But I don't. I just watch him struggle.

"Rebekah!"

What if he just blew away like a kite?

I get tired of waiting, though, so I meet him halfway. I hold onto a pole, and he holds onto me.

"Heaven's gone. I killed them I think. It was a miscalculation on their part, to engage in violence with me."

Hugh's mouth twitches, then sags on one side. I can feel his frantic thoughts, his fear. His desire. I'm tempted. I could suck the marrow from the bone, so to speak.

"I'd hoped it wouldn't come to that," he says at last, speaking so quietly, though I still hear him, or at least I think I do. Maybe I read his lips.

I don't want to be up here anymore, now that he's here. He's spoiled my solitude. "You've ruined the trip, darling. You've fucked it."

He looks confused, then hurt. His grip loosens, then renews, tighter this time. "Please. Forgive me."

I pull him inside—first the door won't open, then

we nearly fall down the steps. The wind grabs the door, there's no closing it after us. I realize I have my arms around Hugh like he's injured. He's limping, even. I pull away and he almost falls over.

Another door. And another. It's quiet now, except for some ambient moans. I stop. "Let me tell you now," I say, and grab him by the shoulders. "There's nothing to forgive, my love. Nothing for me to forgive, that is."

His mouth twitches, cautiously preparing for a smile. "*Mi cielo . . .*"

"You'll have to forgive yourself. If you can." His mouth yields to mine. I want to strip his skin off.

Instead, I do another tongue twirl and pull back. He holds on to me and here comes another flash of memory, a woman with a wretched face reaching so far her shoulders pop, a terrible cry flying out of her mouth.

My cold cheek to his, kiss kiss.

"Rebekah—"

"Goodbye." And quick as a bat, I'm gone.

DAY 14

So slowly, it seems it will never happen, the ship finally docks. In the dead of night, the *Zorya* unceremoniously turns herself inside out. The passengers are purged, stumbling and sick. They're confused—where are we? Some are limping, others have to be carried. The captain is out there in the flesh, bowing and apologizing to everyone.

I work my way through the mob, slipping closer and closer to escape. And escapades. At one point, I think I hear the ribbon of Heaven's laughter, and I freeze. Can it be? If they're alive, they will hunt me. Haunt me. I'm frightened, but also, I've bested them once. An adversary is not a terrible thing, in the end. It keeps things interesting.

And you? Who knows? Maybe we will meet one day.

At last, I'm standing on the street with nothing in my hands. A car comes, I get in, and off I go into the night.

THE END

Acknowledgements

In the fall of 2019, I was working on a novel about a sophisticated, "intellectual" married couple who meet a third partner on a cruise, and both fall in love with them. Then Covid happened and I didn't want to write about cruise ships anymore. Plus I didn't know where that story was really going. So I shelved the whole thing and continued working on what I thought would be my next published book, which is about witches . . . Well, you'll see.

I don't remember exactly when or how the switch happened, though I'm confident it occurred sometime during the months I was prepping for the Study Coven's Vampires + Cannibals class. I was reading everything interesting I could find on vampires. (Yes, I am a devoted *WWDITS* fan. Thank you to everyone who had anything to do with that show.) Eventually, I recognized the partners on the cruise were emotional vampires. And that the enchanting third party, a so-called unicorn, was actually a magical being.

This was essentially the idea I mentioned in passing to my gifted editor at Creature Publishing, Amanda Manns. She immediately recognized the potential in this baby tooth of a story and decided to take a risk on it, despite having no assurance I could actually write funny. What followed was a fast, gratifying writing process, a respite from wrestling with my opus, and a chance to poke fun at myself and fellow artsy queers. Mandi! Thank you for your insight and vision, and general badassery. You make all of this so much easier, cooler, and more fun. Thank you, thank you.

Cheers of gratitude to my beta readers, my dear friends Rachelle Gonzalez, Deborah Steinberg, and Jensen Sikora—my love, my partner-in-hobbitness, protector, and number-one fan. You three were this book's first enthusiasts! It would not be what it is without your thoughtful feedback and faith.

A thousand thanks to Pick Your Potions' Study Coven. You witches gave me a reason to pursue and study vampires in the first place, but more importantly, your innovative and at times hilariously profane work has taught me a great deal about how to craft a killer story. It's an honor and a privilege to guide this group onward into the weird.

Eternal gratitude to Anne Rice, who is no longer on this plane. Mistress of dark writing, hear my prayer! *Interview with the Vampire* was my first-ever vampire read. I was twelve years old, sexually frustrated, and enthralled by the teasing homoeroticism on the page, and Rice's general over-the-topness in life. I mean, *there's* a role model. Still, I spent a few decades of my early writing life trying to produce "serious stories." Genre writers weren't respected in my MFA program, and magic was ok only if you could do it like Karen Russell. But I kept drifting into witches and ghosts. At that time, I had never heard the term "feminist horror." *Beloved* was (and remains) one of my favorite novels, but I never thought of it as a ghost story. So I went on, not seeing myself, underestimating the importance of my exposure to Rice in making me the writer I became.

And now, I embrace the monsters.

I reread *Interview* a few years ago. I admit I was prepared for disappointment. I didn't expect it to live up to memory. Instead, I found a complex, undeniably literary work of horror. It was artful in its terror, both erotic and provocative. I highly recommend giving it another look.

Finally, to all the readers, including the blurbers and their confidence-boosting praise, I say, thank you, there is no point to all this without you. Cheers!

LINDSAY MERBAUM is a queer author of strange tales and the founder of Pick Your Potions, a consortium of mixology and witchery. Her first novel with Creature Publishing, *The Gold Persimmon*, was a 2021 Foreword Indies Finalist. Lindsay lives in Michigan with her partner and cats.

CREATURE PUBLISHING was founded on a passion for feminist discourse and horror's potential for social commentary and catharsis. Our definition of feminist horror, broad and inclusive, expands the scope of what horror can be and who can make it.